Ghost Me Once

by

K. M. Daughters

Ghost Me Once

Cover Art by *Lisa Dawn MacDonald*

The Wild Rose Press, Inc.
PO Box 708
Adams Basin, NY 14410-0708
Visit us at www.thewildrosepress.com

Publishing History
First Edition, 2025
Trade Paperback Print ISBN 978-1-5092-6365-3
Digital ISBN 978-1-5092-6366-0

Published in the United States of America

Dedication

To Mom. Thank you for making us the strong women and mothers we are today.

Chapter 1

"Who do you think *he* is?" Brooke couldn't tear her eyes away from the tall, *very* well-built man on a ladder in front of the café.

He presented his back to them as he worked to reattach the corner of a flapping awning. Walnut colored hair cut just below his ears curled around the band of a backwards baseball cap. His jeans fit perfectly over taut buns. He stretched his arms up overhead, causing his white T-shirt to ride up to the middle of his back. His impressive musculature and tanned skin instantly attracted Brooke. He was either a gym rat—a man after her own heart—or he was amply genetically blessed.

"My guess is Jaxson Rosso, the owner's son himself," Mike said. "Aside from a part time cook, he and his mother are the only employees at Pops' Café according to the case file."

Brooke pointed to a Help Wanted sign in the window. "They're looking to add employees. This may be easier than we thought. Let's go have some breakfast and scope things out."

Mike made to open the front door for his partner but halted when the man on the ladder called down to them, "Am I in your way, here? I'm almost done and can move the ladder if you give me a sec."

Brooke smiled and waved off his offer. "We have enough room to skootch in through the door. This your

1

place?"

He wagged his head. "No. It's my mother's restaurant inherited from her father." He tilted his head toward the restaurant's signage. "My granddad was Pops. Welcome. I'll be inside in a few minutes to take your breakfast orders."

Brooke ducked under Mike's arm and entered the cheerful restaurant bustling despite the early hour on a sleepy California Sunday. A petite, brunette woman who was seated behind the front counter popped up and greeted them with a sunny smile, hand outstretched. "I'm Sofia Baxter. Welcome for the first time to Pops'."

Suspect number two in the same place. How convenient.

Brooke returned Sofia's soft handshake. "Nice to meet you, Sofia. I'm Brooke James and this is my brother Mike James. How do you know it's our first time here?"

The owner chuckled. "This is a small place in a small town, and I know everyone who walks through my front door. Are you vacationing in Luna Beach?" Sofia picked up two laminated menus and moved out from behind the counter.

"No," Brooke said. "My brother and I just moved here from Virginia yesterday."

"Wow. One coast to the other; that's a major move." Sofia set in motion into the cozy dining room.

Brooke noted her slow, purposeful gait. Documented in the case file, Sofia had suffered a heart attack a few weeks ago which had brought her son from New York to California to help her out. He had taken a three-month leave of absence from his upper echelon position with a prestigious accounting firm to run the restaurant while his mom fully recovered.

Sofia led Brooke and Mike to the only empty booth overlooking the street which provided Brooke with a tantalizing view of Jaxson Rosso dismounting the ladder out front. He caught her peering through the window and gave her a wink, his crystal blue eyes twinkling silver.

Oh, she almost exclaimed aloud. Impossible, but the man viewed from straight-on was even more a feast for her eyes than from behind. He collapsed the ladder, hoisted it up with one arm displaying an impressive bicep bulge, and then walked away from the front of the building to, she assumed, the back door of the restaurant.

Brooke followed his progress with dreamy absorption. When he disappeared from view, she turned her attention back to Sofia who regarded her with an amused expression. Who knows how long she had held the menu out in Brooke's direction while she ignored her and ogled her son?

She mentally shook off her distraction with Jaxson and accepted the menu from Sofia. Back to business.

"What do you recommend, Sofia?"

"I think you'll find you can't go wrong no matter what you choose."

"Go with the Pops' Special. I order that every day," came a husky male voice from behind her.

Brooke turned and faced the speaker, a burly surfer dude draping his tattooed arm over the back of the booth, sporting a durag and a wide grin.

"If you don't mind my saying so, you are the prettiest lady I have ever seen in my life."

He extended a beefy paw.

Brooke hesitated to accept the handshake.

"Don't mind Duke, Brooke. He's harmless— mostly."

Taking the owner at her word, Brooke gave Duke's hand a light shake. "Nice to meet you."

"You, too. Thanks for the vote of confidence, Sof."

Sofia patted his arm, chuckling. "You know I love you. I better go sit down before my son tells me to."

Jaxson Rosso appeared in the dining room snagging Brooke's attention again. "Ma, get off your feet," he boomed.

"Yeah, yeah. I'm going, Jax." Sofia shot a grin at him and then turned to face Brooke. "Have a nice breakfast."

Brooke enjoyed watching Jax effortlessly take orders and chat up the patrons with a contagious smile on his handsome face. The bio that her team had put together had failed to mention that the man was flat out gorgeous.

"Stop staring. You're drooling." Mike abruptly cut off her gawking.

She glared at Mike and gave him a rapid-fire jab.

"Ow." He rubbed his arm. "What the heck…"

"Lover's quarrel? I can come back."

Brooke jumped at the sound of the bass voice and looked away from Mike. Jax, in all his hunky glory, stood at their table, coffee carafe in hand.

"Ew." She grimaced with a shiver. "He's my brother."

"Good to know." He looked deeply into her eyes and grinned as if she had given him the best news, stirring a swell of attraction in her core.

"Ready to order?" Jax said.

Mike handed the menus to Jax. "We'll both have the Pops' Special. But hold the bacon on hers. Bacon always makes my sister fart."

Brooke's jaw dropped, and a hot blush bloomed on her cheeks. Jax let out a belly laugh that had heads turning toward them in the dining room.

Mike casually scrolled on his phone, his eyes downturned, as if he hadn't embarrassed the hell out of her.

Brooke jabbed Mike's arm again with closed-fisted gusto.

Coffee?" Jax was straight-faced, but Brooke could read playful amusement in his eyes.

"Oh yes, please," she said.

Jax filled Brooke's mug. "How about you?" He arched his eyebrows at Mike.

"Yeah, thanks," Mike said.

"I'll go get your orders started and bring a bread basket. Do either of you want anything else to drink? We have a variety of juices."

"I'm good with coffee," Brooke said.

"Me, too." Mike pointed to the carafe. "Maybe you could you leave that on the table?"

Jax set the pot down. "Of course. Your meal will be out shortly. By the way, you deserved that punch." Jax laughed all the way back to the kitchen.

****

The woman had scrambled his thoughts from the moment he had caught sight of her. Jax had almost lost his footing on the ladder looking down on her crown of glossy ebony hair framing a perfect face highlighted by glimmering emerald eyes. Bewitching. Stunning.

He strode into the kitchen, gave the siblings' orders to Sergio, plucked a plastic basket off a shelf, lined it with a napkin and filled it with assorted breads. Jax grabbed a full pot of coffee off the stove, delivered the basket to Brooke's table, and made the rounds topping off customers' Pops' Café insignia mugs, his eyes straying to the beautiful stranger who was so lovely, she didn't seem real. More like every man's dream girl.

She had jet black, waist length hair which she wore straight, a shiny cascade over her shoulders and down her back. He only had a brief glimpse of her figure outside the café, but that was long enough to appreciate her lithe body, long shapely legs and toned arms in her sleeveless, yellow top and black shorts. At the first sight of her, he was left wanting to get close to her. Jax had never had such an electric attraction to a woman. Not even after becoming involved romantically in the past.

Case in point—Sandra. He was certain she had already moved out of his condo in New York after a two-year relationship. Her reason for dumping him still stung. She had heatedly accused him of being a mama's boy if he had chosen to leave her to help his ailing mother. Sandra had made it clear that if he decided in favor of Sofia and left for California, she wouldn't be there when he returned. Her coldness and lack of understanding could never generate the blast of attraction that the virtual stranger had set off in him.

He bussed vacated tables, doled out coffee, and managed the breakfast rush like a pro. The past weeks, Jax had remembered the restaurateur's choreography that he had learned from his beloved granddad from an early age.

Jax missed working with Pops, especially when he was back home in California away from his demanding, consuming corporate job in NYC. He missed Pops in general. He was more father to Jax than grandfather since his biological father had abandoned his pregnant mother before Jax was born. The languishing business at the café was confined to mostly breakfast on weekends since Pops' death despite Jax's advertising that they were open for lunch, too, seven days a week. Even though the place was far from profitable, Jax fully understood his mother's desire to keep the doors open in her father's memory. He had no problem sending her money each month to keep the place alive even though he resented his stepfather's refusal to do so. Jax detested his stepfather and his detached treatment of his mother and wanted nothing to do with him.

A bell dinged, alerting Jax that food was up and ready to serve. He strode over to the pass-through counter. The order was for the squabbling siblings, so he gladly toted the full tray over to their table to get another eyeful of Brooke. He set the array of dishes in front of each of them.

She widened her eyes. "Yum. Bacon."

Jax grinned. "Extra bacon."

"Thank you for ignoring my block head brother. I do *not* pass gas eating bacon."

"Do, too." Mike put his phone down, took both his arms off the table top and rested his hands in his lap, presumably preventing his sister's punches.

She wagged her head at Mike and then pinned Jax with her round, lawn-green eyes holding him in her thrall. "This seems like such a friendly place. I'm glad we happened upon it our first morning in Luna Beach."

"Glad you chose to come in for breakfast. We haven't been formally introduced. I'm Jax Rosso. You've already met my mother and the owner of Pops' Café."

"Good to meet you, Jax. I'm Brooke James." She

placed her hand in his for a shake.

Her touch brought a sensual surge that had him holding her hand a few beats longer than the handshake required. She gave him a sly smile that told him she felt the connection, too.

"By the way, I'm Mike James," her brother interjected.

Jax shifted his handshake from Brooke to Mike. "Nice to meet you."

"Would you like to join us for breakfast, Jax? God knows there's enough here." Brooke waved a hand over the table.

I'd love to but I'm where the buck stops here. Jax smiled.

"No thanks. I still have work to do. But no worries. I have plenty of to-go boxes. Enjoy your meal."

Chapter 2

He left the brother and sister to their breakfasts and decided to have a talk with his mom to learn more about Brooke. Jax was positive she'd have gleaned information chatting Brooke up, like she did all the customers. He rounded the front counter and leaned against it nonchalantly.

Better to be straightforward with her since she had a very accurate BS detector. "What can you tell me about the James siblings?"

She narrowed her brown eyes. Jax sensed that she knew full well that he was interested in learning about only one of the two siblings. "They've moved here from Virginia for Mike to start a job. So they're not tourists."

"Okay. Anything else?"

"Nope." Sofia picked up a pile of menus and banged them into alignment on the counter.

"But if I were you, I'd ask Brooke if she'd like you to show her around town. Since you know Luna Beach like the back of your hand, and you'd be doing her a community service welcoming her and all." She gave him a wide smile.

Jax twisted his lips and chuckled. "Yes, Ma, I *am* interested in her. Can't pull the wool over your eyes for sure."

"Always a step ahead of you, son."

He stood upright and made to return to his work.

She touched his sleeve. "By the way. She was watching you like a hawk when you took the ladder down outside. I'd say she's interested in you, too."

That opinion was more than welcome. "Thanks, Ma. I'll go finish the breakfast service and set the tables for lunch."

"Why bother. Noone comes…"

True, he thought as he returned to the dining room. But maybe his advertising would eventually pay off.

Jax drifted past Brooke's booth on his way to the kitchen.

"Jax, do you have a minute?" she called out.

For you I have hours. "Sure." He reversed and walked over to her booth.

"My brother and I just moved to Luna Beach because Mike landed his dream job here. Our parents are gone, and nothing was keeping me back home in Virginia, so I decided to move, too. I've never been to California before, and I was up for an adventure. I'm looking for work and I noticed the Help Wanted sign in your window. Can I please apply?"

He couldn't contain a grin at her request. The fates were smiling on him. "We really don't have a formal application process. I can't guarantee full time hours. Also, we can only manage to pay minimum wage. Still interested?"

"I am."

"That's great. Uh…we have to run this by my mother. I'm sure she won't object. By the way, do you have experience as a food server?"

"No. Unless you count working in the hospital cafeteria as a volunteer Candy Striper when I was fourteen."

He laughed. "I'll count it. Hang on a minute. I'll bring my mother over to talk with you."

Jax strode back to the front of the restaurant. "Ma, Brooke wants the part-time server job. Are you okay with that?"

"More than okay. That woman is daughter-in-law material. This is *great*. When can she start?"

"Don't go getting ahead of yourself." He couldn't help but laugh at his matchmaker mom. She was highly vocal about how often she dreamed of being a grandmother. "You can get the details from her. So you know, she doesn't really have experience."

"Well then, you'll have to work *closely* with her to teach her what your pops taught you."

He rolled his eyes and left his mother to finalize details with Brooke.

"The job is yours," Jax told Brooke. "When can you start?"

"Tomorrow if that's okay? This is great."

"Perfect. Are you done with your food?"

Both Brooke and Mike nodded.

"Couldn't eat another bite," she said.

"We are proud of our portions," Jax said. "I'll take your plates in back and box them for you. By the way…" He placed their plates on a tray and directed his gaze toward Mike. "What's the dream job that brought you coast to coast?"

Mike leaned forward, a delighted expression on his face as if he had pulled the career brass ring. "Tomorrow I'll be an Engineer for Mercury Labs. Programming, coding, artificial intelligence, etc. That's my field. I've wanted to work at Mercury since I got my graduate degree."

"Mercury Labs?" Thurston Baxter's, his detested stepfather's, corporate kingdom.

"Good luck with *that*," Jax spat out. He hoisted the tray and marched into the kitchen.

****

"Well *that* was telling." Brooke leaned back in her seat looking across the table at Mike. "I want to investigate what he meant by that and stick around. Are you okay with paying the check and meeting me back at the apartment?"

Mike pulled a wallet out of his back pocket. "I can do that. But I'd be happier about hanging out there if the pool were actually filled with water and the place didn't smell like mildew. You'd think my star pupil at Quantico and Daddy's little girl would rate better digs."

He smiled warmly at her, delivering that last jab, but it rankled anyway.

"Let's not get into the nepotism thing, okay? You, of all people know that I earned Special Agent In Charge with hard work and the director had nothing to do with it."

"I do. You were in my training class, and you earned every point with drive and excellence, exactly what the Bureau is looking for. Don't forget, I requested that you partner with me on this Op."

Brooke scooted out of the booth and grinned down at Mike. "But I'll bet you thought my father would give us first class beach digs, right?"

"Maybe."

She burst out laughing. "I'll see you later. I'm going to the kitchen to tell Jax there's no time like the present to start training. Maybe he'll be in a talkative mood. It seems like he's not a fan of Thurston Baxter, head honcho at Mercury Labs."

"Sounds good. I'll just open some windows to try to air the place out and call Kay."

"Give her my love."

Brooke moved away from the booth on a bead toward the kitchen when Duke called out, "Where are you going, Fabulosa? The door is that way."

She sidestepped to face him. "Fabulosa? What the heck is that?"

"Only way to describe you. Unless you prefer Babe."

"Neither. Ugh. Thanks for the effort, though." Brooke knit her brows but gave him a smile anyway. She agreed with Sofia. He was mostly harmless.

She swung into the kitchen and bumped straight into Jax's chest.

"Oof," he said, although it was only a gentle collision.

Brooke backed up. "That couldn't have possibly knocked the breath out of you."

Jax's face lit with a broad grin. His dancing blue eyes flecked with silver mesmerized her. "More like you took my breath away."

"Oh…" She lowered her gaze to the floor, charmed by Jax, despite that she should remain objective and covertly interrogate him.

No harm in enjoying the view and the banter. Right?

Confident that she could handle him, she assumed the role of an anxious to please new employee. "My brother left, but I thought I could stick around and get a jump on learning the ropes around here…no need to pay me yet, and only if you're not too busy to give me some pointers, that is."

"No, uh…here." He handed her a stack of Styrofoam containers. "These are your leftovers. We have logo plastic bags in that bin over there. Bag these and then you can shadow me in the dining room."

"Sure."

She passed by a man standing at the massive griddle wielding a spatula who shot Jax a quizzical expression.

"Brooke, meet Sergio. Sergio, this is Brooke, our new part-time server."

"Hi, Sergio. I'm looking forward to working with you."

He waggled his eyebrows at Jax. "Me, too with you."

Brooke completed the first menial task of bagging the containers, set them on the counter to take with her later and fell in line behind Jax out into the dining room. She'd prefer sitting across a table from him and engaging him in useful conversation, but there'd be time for that. Her first priority was to pay attention to Jax's direction. As with any job Brooke undertook, she had to excel. She would become the perfect server.

The customers that Jax introduced were self-described as regulars, so Brooke memorized names and faces preparing to personalize her future interactions with them. To the last person, everyone was welcoming and friendly which surprised her. Apparently the stereotype of a southern Californian as aloof and self-involved—the types that wouldn't wave, say hello or good morning if you passed them hiking or jogging—was a misconception. Already she felt embraced by the cheerful atmosphere of Pops' Café.

The job was a convenient cover to surveille Jax and

Sofia that she had seized as a means to an end. She hadn't expected to enjoy it during her time in Luna Beach.

The customers drifted out of the restaurant almost simultaneously. Jax explained that the regulars waited for him and his mother to unlock the door at six a.m., generally ordered the same food every day, ate heartily and chatted up table neighbors, dabbed their mouths with napkins and departed. Same deal every day.

"That's wonderful that you have so much repeat business." Brooke followed Jax to the kitchen to unload the last tray of dirty dishes.

"It is," he said.

"Are they the same regulars for lunch, too?"

"Nope." He held the swinging kitchen door open for her.

"Oh. So I'll meet new regulars in…" She glanced at her smart watch. "A couple hours?"

"I wish. No regulars at lunch. Hardly any customers at all for lunch. I'm still grappling with how to attract them." He took her tray, placed it on the counter, opened the door of the industrial dishwasher and stooped, loading it.

Brooke pitched in. Jax set the dials to wash and then faced her.

"No need to stick around today, Brooke…or every day after the breakfast customers are taken care of. Unless you have time to sit with me over a cup of coffee on the house?"

Perfect. "That sounds great. Thanks."

Jax poured their drinks and preceded her out of the kitchen, propping his back against the door to hold it open for her.

She breezed by him catching a whiff of the musky,

aphrodisiac aftershave that he wore.

Seated across from him in the same booth that she and Mike had shared, she marveled at how much more she enjoyed looking at Jax than at Mike.

"Can I ask you a question about your conversation with my brother earlier?" she said.

"Sure. What do you want to know?"

Brooke already knew what his answer would be in general terms since she knew from his bio in the case file that Baxter was his stepfather. But Jax didn't know that she knew. And she wanted to see how deeply connected he was to Baxter and Mercury Labs.

"Did I misread kind of a snarky reaction to Mike's telling you about his new job?"

He twisted his lips and stirred some milk into his coffee mug. "I guess it was snarky. But I didn't mean to diminish Mike's excitement about his dream job. I know the chief executive of that company personally and frankly I can't stand him."

"I don't understand," she lied. "How do you have anything to do with Mercury Labs? They're involved in AI. That's one of Mike's specialties as he mentioned."

"I'm not involved with the company at all. Frankly, I don't know a thing about what they do there. Thurston Baxter, if you're familiar with that name, is my stepfather."

"Wow. I only know what's been reported about him in the media. Sofia is so down to earth. You'd never know that she's married to a tech billionaire."

"Yeah, well. He puts a roof over her head. Their house, which he bought without a shred of input from my mom since he didn't deign to even show her the place before buying it, is a showplace. Architectural Digest shoots and all that. He manages the help staff who he has directed to only take orders from him and generally doesn't give my mother a dime that she doesn't have to beg for. The SOB won't help her financially to keep this place going. It means the world to her, and he doesn't care. I can't stand the guy."

"He sounds like a tyrant. Why did a sweet woman like your mother marry him in the first place?"

"That's a long story that we'll save for another time."

"Okay." Brooke backed away from that line of questioning. "I don't mean to pry."

"You're not. Anything else you'd like to know?"

"Yes. With the business in trouble, how *does* she keep this place going?"

"I send her some money every month. It's really nothing and I'd give her just about any amount, but she insists that she can keep the lights on with it. I won't let her lose this business that was so special to Pops and the family."

On impulse, Brooke covered his warm hand with hers. "You're a good man, Jax."

A slow smile bloomed on his lips. He really was breathtaking. And Brooke was convinced that every word he had said was true. So as sweet as she appeared, Sofia had to be Baxter's co-traitor.

Brooke finished the last sip of coffee. "I'll leave now if there's nothing else you'd like me to do."

"No. That will about do it for today. Be here at 5:45 tomorrow morning. I'll have a set of keys made for you this afternoon."

"Great. I'll be here. And Jax…?"

"Yes?"

17

"Thank you for the job."

"You're very welcome. You did good today. Maybe you haven't forgotten your Candy Striper days."

Brooke hooted a laugh and grabbed the to go containers. "See you in the morning."

Chapter 3

Brooke pounded on the door of her temporary apartment wondering what the heck was taking Mike so long to open up. She made a mental note to grab his keys when she got inside, find a hardware store and have a set made so she could come and go as she pleased.

She continued banging until the door finally swung open with a squeal of the hinges. Mike appeared in the doorway holding his cell phone in hand with his ear buds plugged in. "Kay," he mouthed.

She nodded and stepped inside the dingy living room. A skimpy kitchen counter with a couple of rickety bar stools pulled up to it was dead ahead. An ancient microwave and coffee maker perched on the counter next to the sink that no amount of steel wool could clean. The refrigerator was circa early millennia whirring a little too loudly for Brooke to think it would survive their stay there. There wasn't even an oven. Just a two-burner hot plate. She was an adequate cook and Mike claimed he was an excellent one. But nothing but takeout and whatever they might eat at the café was in their future.

Mike sat at a parlor-sized table on one of the two chairs in the place with his legs outstretched and propped up on the other chair talking to his fiancée and Brooke's best friend from childhood. Kay had met Mike visiting Brooke at Quantico and it was love at first sight for both of them. They'd yet to set a wedding date, but Brooke had already accepted Kay's request to be her Maid of Honor. She was thrilled at the privilege.

"Put the call on speaker phone so I can say hi," she said.

He switched the phone's audio and placed it down on the table. "Brooke wants to say hello."

"Hey girl. How's that California sunshine? All it's cracked up to be?" Kay said.

Brooke waved Mike's feet off the chair and took a seat. "Not a lot of sunshine streaming through this apartment's tiny window, but it is pretty outside. Warm and breezy. If we don't stay inside this horrible apartment, we're golden. You should see it, Kay. It's so subpar I'm afraid to touch anything. I refused to let my body brush anywhere near the walls of the shower. Awful."

"You neglected to tell Kay about the pool," Mike said.

"Oh yeah. It's pure grunge on the bottom and completely drained. There's a couple of pool chairs scattered around that probably wouldn't hold a toddler's weight," Brooke said.

"Yuck, you guys. I'm so sorry," Kay said. "How long do you think you'll be there? Or is it top secret?"

"As long as it takes, sweetheart. As long as it takes," Mike said.

"Don't worry," Brooke chimed in. "I'll work my tail off to get out of here."

"Me, too. Can't get back to you soon enough."

Brooke gazed at the cell phone as if she could see Kay's pretty face on the screen. "Are you sure you want him back? This guy is OCD big time. He's been on me since we arrived yesterday. Put this away. Unpack now.

Don't leave this or that lying around. Don't kick off your shoes and just leave them there. Stack those papers and put them where they belong. Blah, blah. You'll go crazy living with this neatnik."

Mike rolled his eyes as Kay burst out laughing. "We've struck a nice balance whenever we stay together."

"Yeah but…" Brooke continued. "When you marry him, this will be for life."

"Oh shut up." Mike's tone was good natured. He took the call off the speaker.

"Hey," Brooke protested. "I didn't get to say goodbye."

"Brooke says goodbye."

Wagging her head, Brooke rose from the chair and traipsed out of the living area down a narrow hallway, past Mike's room, the tiny hall bathroom, and into her bedroom, identical to Mike's. A thin truly ugly coverlet in a pukey shade "adorned" the twin bed. One prison-sized window provided daylight. Mike had opened the window to air out the place and Brooke noticed the myriad of pinholes in the screen. Good thing California wasn't too heavy on mosquito population.

She lifted her briefcase off the top of a scratched wooden, three door chest and sat down on the bed with it. Extracting the Op Case File, she perused the classified contents for the umpteenth time: bios on generations of Jax's family, bank statements, background on Mercury Labs and Baxter's employment records, phone records, assorted photographs of suspicious meetings with foreign adversaries, and records of electronic transfers of large sums. The three principal suspects in the case were Jax, Sofia and Thurston. It was the DOJ's contention that the entire family was involved in the treason.

Mike played a critical role in the investigation to gather the electronic evidence that would lead to convictions. He was an expert on so many fronts and a respected Quantico instructor. He rarely did field work, but in this case, his know-how was crucial. When they got closer to corroborating the facts in the case, a tactical ops team would join them. Possibly they'd request the team sooner if electronic surveillance of the suspects' residences was necessary.

Bent over the file, Brooke didn't notice Mike standing in the doorway. "Want to go over that together?"

She startled briefly. "Um…sure."

"Let's spread out on the table…so to speak," he said.

File in hand, Brooke followed Mike out into the kitchen and took a seat at the table opposite him. They opened identical files.

"Let's look at Jax first, okay?" Brooke proposed.

Mike nodded agreement.

"Nothing remarkable in his early years," Brooke read. "He confirmed a lot of what's here in our conversation at Pops' Café this morning. Raised by his mother and abandoned before birth by his father. His grandfather, who he called Pops, was a prominent father figure in his life. He worked at the café with Pops after school from age sixteen up until leaving for college. He earned a Bachelor of Sciences degree from the University of Alabama. A baseball star there with a championship team. Majored in Economics and landed his New York job with Allen & Forbes straight out of school, graduating Summa Cum Laude. He used the company's tuition reimbursement benefit and earned a

Masters' Degree from NYU. He was promoted three times to his current position of Director of Accounting. Possible partnership in the firm might be in his future.

"Jax took a leave when Sofia suffered a heart attack. The terms of the leave are to use up paid personal time off and vacation pay before going unpaid in a couple months. His bank records show low six figure savings and $5,000.00 monthly payments sent to his mother, purpose unknown per the file.

"I learned today that he sends Sofia money to keep the café operating. No mystery there. Also, no record of money flowing from her to him. No red flags on his financials overall. They're within the bounds of his $450,000.00, plus bonus yearly income.

"I also learned today that he loathes Thurston Baxter and has nothing to do with him. I don't know the full story, but I will soon."

She flipped a page. "And then there's Sofia."

"Yep," Mike said. "The keeper of the family treasury. So far she's amassed fifty million. The regularity of ETF deposits is irregular. But we're talking large sums each time a transfer is made."

Brooke leaned back in her chair, eyes off the file. "Boy, I'm having a hard time attaching her to this level of subterfuge. I realize I just met her, but she seems like an open book and not some sort of secret femme fatale."

"I agree with your assessment, but we have to assume she's up to her neck in this. And if she is, Jax is, too."

Brooke nodded and gazed down at the file again. She picked up a few of the photographs. "Have you identified these guys with Baxter?"

"Not yet. The meetings with these apparent Chinese

nationals might not be attached to the money in Sofia's account, although I'm ninety-nine percent sure that I will find that they are. The corporation does a lot of business in China. The newly built AI warehouse on the outskirts of Beijing might owe its operating capability to Baxter selling them the know-how. National security breach written all over this if I can prove the connection. The corporation's ties to the country are firmly established."

"Yet, Baxter's financials are squeaky clean." Brooke consulted the file.

"Right. But the big money isn't coming to him directly. It's all siphoned through Sofia."

She closed the file. "Are you going anywhere for about an hour? I'd like to make a set of keys."

"Help yourself. They're over there on the counter. Do you want to rent a car for yourself? The budget can handle it."

"No thanks. I'm walking distance from the café and that's where I'll be most of the time. If anything changes, I'll let you know."

Mike nodded. "I think I'll check out the NFL on that miniature TV in there." He pointed to the offensive appliance.

"Maybe put a towel or something down on that sofa before you sit on it."

He arched his eyebrows. "Maybe I'll just stay right here and stream the games on my computer."

Brooke huffed a laugh. "Good plan. I'll be back soon."

"Before you leave, please stow your case file in your room."

"Yes, Felix. Right away."

Mike chuckled. "Thanks, Oscar."

She obeyed her superior officer and then scooped the keys off the counter and headed to the rental car. In the driver seat she opened her maps app and searched hardware stores. The nearest was a fifteen-minute drive, fastest route. She chose the longer route that would take her down Pacific Coast Highway and rolled down her window anticipating the lovely breeze driving along the oceanfront. Placing her AirPods in her ears, she put the car in gear.

California really was beautiful. She loved the climate in Virginia near the Chesapeake Bay, but the consistently mild weather in Southern California had her home town beat. The AI assistant navigated her to the hardware store, and she parked and went inside. A high school aged boy with an unfortunately pimply face lingered at the key grinding machine longer than necessary in a valiant attempt to flirt with her. Despite the futility of his efforts, she left the store smiling at the compliment.

Back behind the wheel, she decided to drive around and explore the area for a while. Mostly to delay returning to her dismal apartment. She *could* join Mike in watching football. Brooke loved the football season and gladly spent the money for the NFL Sunday ticket every year. One of the few cozy father-daughter memories that she cherished was watching football for the first time with her military-like dad. He taught her the rules of the game and playfully bet a dollar against her pick to win—the Green Bay Packers. Since her team mostly won, he filled her piggy bank. She had never lost her devotion to Green Bay all those years since. And they were playing later. But, staying inside on a day like today would bring cabin fever for sure.

Her cell phone trilled. She responded to the AI voice to accept the call from her father, the Director of the FBI himself.

"Hello, sir. How are things in Washington?"

"I haven't slept in twenty-four hours."

And probably looking fresh and starched and eagle-eyed as usual. "Anything I should be aware of that's robbing you of rest, sir?"

"It's all connected. But I have nothing to add to the Case File at this time. How are you and Mike getting along?"

She smiled thinking about her clean freak temporary roommate. "Very well. We're settled in and have already begun surveillance of two of the suspects. They work in the same restaurant. Pops Café. As you know. Fate has it that they were looking for help. I officially start work there tomorrow as a server."

"Excellent. Mike all set, too?"

"Absolutely. He starts at Mercury tomorrow. He's already been issued his security badge."

"He's a good man. Pride of the Bureau."

"Yes, sir, he is. I'm honored to partner with him."

Aren't you going to say I'm a good "man", too. Your pride and joy and all that? No. You certainly are not.

"I'm sure you'll do well. You have my blood running in your veins, after all."

"That is true, sir. I'm very fortunate to have you as a role model."

Would she never talk to her dad the way Sofia and Jax talked to each other? Like loving family and not…robots? Dad always had wanted a son. Mom died before he could overcome the apparent trauma of only having a female child. But he did a good job raising her like the son he would never have. Despite her resentment of that truth, Brooke loved her father unconditionally. And she would fulfill his every wish for her. And never, ever complain.

"Are the living accommodations adequate?"

Hardly. "Yes, sir. They are."

"Good. I'll follow your progress closely."

"Thank you, sir."

He disconnected the call.

"And have a nice day and I miss you and love you, Brooke," she proclaimed to nobody. "Love you, too, Dad," she whispered.

The joy having gone out of her ride, she decided to return to the apartment and watch football after all. On the way she passed by Pops' Café and a rush of anticipation of seeing Jax and digging in to her part of the investigation surged.

Back at "Deluxe Apartment Homes" per the totally inaccurate sign, she parked and used her new key to open their unit's door.

"Get your keys made?" Mike tossed out over his shoulder from the couch.

He had followed her advice and had covered the sofa cushion that he sat on with a mostly threadbare beach towel.

"Yep. Who do you want in the next game, Green Bay or Chicago?" she said.

"Da Bears all the way."

She grinned. "Good. I want Green Bay. Care to put your money where your mouth is?"

"Ten bucks?"

"It's a bet. Let me go find a towel to sit on."

Chapter 4

Brooke paid and tipped the delivery boy just as the third quarter of the football game had begun. The Bears were up by sixteen points sinking Brooke into a dark mood. But, the aroma of the Chinese takeout had her smiling anyway in anticipation of the meal.

She grabbed two seen-better-days plates and some silverware and plopped the bags of food on the bare bones coffee table, handed Mike a bottle of water and then sat down next to him.

Brooke bit into her favorite crab Rangoon, let out a satisfied moan as she chewed, and leaned back into the drab brown, uncomfortable couch.

Even though it was only a preseason game, Brooke cheered as if Green Bay had won the Super Bowl when the game ended. In the last second a successful field goal brought the win for the Packers. She held her hand open in front of Mike's face until he dug in his pocket, pulled out a ten-dollar bill and begrudgingly placed it in her palm.

"The Bears will beat you when it counts," he mumbled.

"Want to make another bet?" she teased.

He narrowed his eyes and wagged his head, Bears loyalty only going so far.

"I'm stuffed." She cleared their plates and stowed the leftovers in the fridge.

"I think I'll get a run in before bedtime. I have to be at work early, so I won't get a chance in the morning. Do you want to come?"

Brooke assumed Mike would refuse to join her since he avoided working out as much as he could. She was right.

"That sounds like an awful idea," he said predictably. He leaned back on the couch and rubbed his flat stomach. "I'm just going to sit here like a blob and watch the next game."

She chuckled. "You do you."

Brooke dressed in her favorite jogging gear: leggings with two side pockets and a matching crop top. She slid her phone into one of the pockets on her thigh and placed her earbuds in her ears.

Mike was snoozing on the couch when she returned to the living room. She put on her aviator sunglasses and tiptoed out the door, pocketing the front door key. With a run on the beach in mind, she headed down a street which she thought might eventually lead to the ocean. At the end of a lane, a staircase led down to the sand.

The sun had started to dip low along the horizon igniting scattered clouds with a tangerine glow. Brooke stood drinking in the vista forgetting for the moment her career, the investigation and her father's expectations of her for the first time since arriving in California.

She set the timer on her smart watch for a half hour and headed back when the alarm sounded. The sun setting over the Pacific seemed to set the ocean on fire painting the sky with crimson and magenta flames.

Brooke turned away from the water and headed toward the stairs.

Footfalls pounded behind her. "Brooke is that you?"

Brooke pivoted rapidly at the sound of a man's voice and crashed into Jax. He reached out and held on to her shoulders to steady her.

"Jax, you scared me." She clutched her hand to her chest and took her earbuds out of her ears.

"I'm sorry. I thought I recognized you when I left my condo, and I called your name a few times. You set a mean pace."

"I didn't hear you." She showed him the ear buds in the palm of her hand. "I didn't know you lived on the beach." *Liar.*

"My grandparents lived here for thirty years. Pops left the condo to me. Want to walk with me for a while or are you done for the day?"

"Let's walk. It's so pretty here. Grandparents are the best aren't they?" Brooke fell into step next to Jax enjoying his nearness and forgetting that where Jax was concerned, she needed to focus on work versus pleasure. "My Nana, my mom's mom, left me the family home on the Chesapeake Bay when she passed away," she said.

Her heart raced the minute she had finished speaking as she realized her error in imparting true personal information to a suspect. Those blues eyes would be her downfall if she dropped her guard again.

"How did you brother feel about that? Wasn't he jealous?"

"Not at all. Nana left him money, and he bought himself a sweet condo. It works out great. I let him use the house and he lets me use the condo." She made a mental note to tell Mike how she had covered up the slip.

The colors in the sky grew dimmer, but still beautiful, as the sun seemed to half submerge in the water. The pair veered away from the shoreline toward the staircase. Brooke sat down on the bottom step. Jax squeezed in next to her, his thigh tight against hers. She enjoyed the close contact a little too much.

"I'm used to sunrise jogs at home. This sunset is truly amazing." She brushed sand off her feet and put on her socks and shoes.

"No more beautiful sight anywhere." Jax stared at her rather than the magnificent sunset in front of them.

Flustered by the implied compliment, Brooke rose up off the step to put some distance between them. "I better get back before it gets too dark."

"I can drive you to your place."

"No thanks. I'm good. I'll see you in the morning, boss."

Brooke mounted the stairs two at a time and jogged down the lane, the time spent with Jax more heart-revving than her cardio workout. Her instincts told her that Jax wasn't a part of his family's criminal activities and maybe she could enjoy her powerful attraction to him…and his to her without sacrificing the investigation.

But that was rookie thinking. Better to get her head straight and avoid being alone with him as much as possible.

****

She didn't sleep well, so the aroma of coffee pulled Brooke to the kitchen like a magnet.

Mike smiled at her and slid an oversized mug of the caffeine-laden elixir across the counter.

"Have I told you lately how much I love you? Kay is such a lucky girl." She closed her eyes and savored the special first sip of morning coffee.

Mike smiled. "I figured you needed a boost for your first day of work. Do you want me to drive you?"

"No I'm good. The walk will help to clear the cobwebs out. As you know mornings are not my strong suit."

"Oh I know. How many times were you late for my eight o'clock class?"

"Thankfully no one kept a record, teach."

"Twenty-seven times." He ducked to avoid the wadded-up paper towel she chucked at him.

"Your brain really is like a computer." She finished her coffee, refilled her mug and then stepped into the bathroom to get ready for work.

Half an hour later, dressed in cotton black pants and a white V-neck T-shirt with her hair in a thick long braid down her back, Brooke was ready.

She turned around with one hand on the front door knob. "I slipped when talking to Jax last evening. I told him our nana left me the house on the Chesapeake and you a sweet condo."

"You talked with him alone?"

"Yeah. I met him on the beach when I was jogging. You were asleep when I got back. Sorry."

"No problem. Good luck today." He checked his watch. "I'm going to Mercury Labs earlier than my official start time."

"Sounds good. See you later."

****

Brooke opened the door of Pops' Café. Butterflies fluttered in her stomach. Since she was sixteen, the first day of any new job had made her nervous. But that day she wasn't nervous about waitressing. The prospect of seeing Jax filled her with nervous energy.

During her sleepless night, Jax had dominated her mind. The man affected her like no one else ever had.

She vowed to keep her distance and maintain objectivity. Taking a deep breath she walked through the door.

Sofia was the only one there with her cell phone pressed to her ear. She gave Brooke a wide smile and held her pointer finger up in the air. "I've got to go, Harry. Just make sure I have the order first thing in the morning."

She disconnected the call and put her phone down on the counter. "Always something. A driver was in an accident. Thank God nothing serious, but our order will be delayed until tomorrow. I'm so glad you're here. Come. Let's go into the kitchen and I'll introduce you to Sergio."

Brooke didn't have a chance to say that she had already met the cook while caught up in Sofia's sweeping wake. The kitchen was large, but the room seemed to shrink when Jax walked in the back door.

"Good morning ladies." He strode towards them. "Ready for your first day, Brooke?"

Did he get even better looking overnight? She managed to nod.

"Let's get you an apron and I'll show you were everything is."

She followed Jax around for fifteen minutes before the first customers streamed in.

"You can use the iPad to take orders—which I favor—or a pad and pen like Mom stubbornly uses. It's up to you."

"I'll manage, thanks." Brooke's exceptional memory ruled out needing to use either.

"All set?"

"Ready." She lifted a full pot of coffee off of the stove and swung through the door out into the dining room.

Brooke felt the heat of Jax's gaze as she went about her work filling coffee cups and making small talk. When Jax started to take orders from seated customers, she stationed at the front desk with Sofia and escorted five older men to a booth.

"Good morning, gentlemen. My name is Brooke." She handed them each a menu. "I'll be your server today. I only ask one thing…"

That snagged the men's attention, and they looked up from their menus.

"This is my first day as a waitress, so please be kind."

A portly guy with snow white hair gave her a full denture grin. "Well we certainly will. It's nice to meet you, Brooke. You sure are prettier than Jax."

"Heck yeah."

"You can say that again, Donald."

"You know, young lady. We've been coming here every morning since Jax was a little boy. We were friends with his pops."

"Would you rather Jax serve you?"

"No," they chorused.

Brooke stifled a laugh. "Then what can I get you, gentlemen?"

She memorized their orders and made to head toward Sergio when one of the men piped up, "Where are you from, Brooke? I think I detect an East coast accent."

"Good ear. I'm from Virginia."

"I hear Virginia is for lovers."

"That's true and I'll tell you a secret." She leaned closer to the table. "I left a trail of them behind who would attest to that."

Laughter rang out behind her.

In the kitchen Brooke conveyed the orders to Sergio, picked up a basket and filled it with bread. Jax came through the doors with an order and grabbed a basket to fill, too.

"A trail of lovers huh?" He arched his eyebrows.

Brooke grinned at him and headed back out the swinging doors.

The morning flew by. Brooke handled the influx of early morning regulars well and gave Jax no room for complaint. She finished wiping down one of the tables when a group of rowdy young guys came in.

"I've got this," Jax said.

"Nope. I can handle this, boss." She grabbed menus and strolled over to their table.

"Good morning. My name is Brooke. I'll be your server today." She handed them menus and waited. "Are you ready to order or should I come back in a few minutes?"

The guy closest to her, who Brooke pegged as the alpha of the group, placed his hand on her rear end and left it there. "Stay right there. I'm Derek. What would you recommend, darling?"

She caught Jax's movement out of the corner of her eye but gave him a subtle wave away.

Brooke whipped out her hand, grabbed a hold of the kid's ear lobe and squeezed. He tried to shake her vise-like grip away, but she held fast.

"Ow!" He dropped his hand off her bottom.

"Well, Derek." She stopped squeezing. "I recommend that you never put your hand on a woman unless she invites you to. I'm sure you mama raised you better than that." Brooke gave his ear a final pinch. "So, are you ready to order?

"Most people order the Pops' Special, but I'd go with the French toast and, of course, with bacon. It is so good."

They all ordered the French toast and bacon, probably afraid of bodily harm if they didn't obey her.

Jax followed her into the kitchen. "Well damn. I know who to call for back up with unruly customers now."

"Anytime boss, anytime."

Chapter 5

Jax admired the way that Brooke had handled the affront. His Brooke. He had known the woman for less than a day, but he felt possessive and exclusively connected to her. Baseless since he hadn't even asked her on a date yet to see if the feeling was mutual. He was pretty sure that he hadn't misread the signals. She seemed interested in him apart from impressing him as her boss. He planned to ask her out after work that day, having thought about little else in his dreamscape the night before.

Watching her retreat in the shadows last evening after meeting her by chance on the beach had left him with a hollow feeling inside. He wanted more with Brooke. More than just working together—although he was enjoying the heck out of working with her.

He couldn't contain his mirth thinking about that guy daring to lay a hand on her. Jax burst out laughing.

"What?" she said.

Jax held out his palm until the fit subsided. "I can't erase the image of your putting a vise on that guy's ear. The expression on his face…priceless."

Brooke beamed back at him. "Yeah, well…"

Ding.

Sergio slid plates of French toast and bacon across the counter. Brooke loaded a tray and hefted it up, propped against her shoulder, one hand flat beneath it.

"Into the lion's den," she said.

She sashayed through the swinging door. The hip action wasn't lost on Jax. Nor his cook.

Sergio let out a low whistle. "Va-va-voom."

"You can say that again." Jax loaded a tray and swung out through the door into the dining room.

The morning rush was upon them and there wasn't an empty booth in the house. Sofia chatted up the customers waiting for tables at the front of the restaurant. A line snaked out the front door. If only lunch were as popular.

He served a table, watching Brooke out of the corner of his eye. Something she said had Lily Levant, the stereotypical battleax octogenarian who punished him with her daily patronage actually chuckling. Brooke may not have on the job experience, but she was a natural at Pops' Café.

"Hey, you boy," Lily bellowed.

Here we go.

Jax Knew better than to ignore the summons. He forced a smile, ambled over to Lily's booth and stood shoulder-to-shoulder with Brooke. "Good morning, Ms. Levant. What can I do for you?"

"Do you do promotions around here?"

"Uh. Not exactly. Why?"

"Because Brooke deserves one, that's why."

"I'm so glad you think so. But there's really not a lot of…upward mobility in a small place like this."

Lily knit her brows and Jax braced for an eruption of expletives or whatever the crone unleashed that morning. She pinned him with her glare. "Then pay her more."

Brooke harumphed, casting her gaze sideways at

Jax, her emerald eyes shining.

"That could be arranged."

Jax wasn't entirely opposed to giving Brooke a raise on her first day. But he wasn't in love with the idea, either.

"Good." Lily fussed with the napkin in her lap. "And I don't want you waiting on me anymore. Only this young lady."

That I'll gladly commit to. "You've got it, ma'am. Anything else I can help you with?"

"No. Go away. I was telling Brooke about my waste of space grandson."

Brooke winked at Jax.

Jax meandered to the front of the café full of sympathy for Lily Levant's grandson and all of her relatives.

He leaned against the front counter and smiled at Sofia. "How long is the waiting list?"

She dipped her eyes to her handwritten sheet of paper. "Ten parties." Sofia beamed at him. "We haven't been this busy in a long time. Do you think Brooke is drawing them in?"

Jax hadn't thought of that. "I don't see how. This is her first day. She's relating to the regulars like a champ, but there hasn't been time to get the word out."

"I don't know about that." Sofia pointed to the right side of the café where a wall of plate glass fronted the street. Passers-by peered through the glass scoping out the place. It seemed that when a man's gaze landed on Brooke, her ebony braid gleaming in the daylight, her trim figure, her long shapely legs and extremely appealing rear view, they rounded the corner and queued up at the front door.

"Huh. I see what you mean." Jax was doubly glad that he had impulsively hired her.

"That girl is a treasure," Sofia said.

She cast her gaze into the dining room where Brooke was loading dirty dishes onto a tray. "Go help her, Jax. Take that tray into the kitchen."

Jax sidled up to the empty booth and insinuated himself into position to take away the heavy tray.

"What are you doing?" Brooke said.

"Giving you some help."

"I've got this." She slid the tray to the edge of the table, lifted it with ease, the toned muscles in her arms flexing, and zipped away with her burden into the kitchen.

All morning Jax had felt like Pops was smiling at him over Brooke's addition to the "family" working in Pops' Café. But letting a lady carry a heavy tray? His grandfather would not have approved.

From his earliest memory, Pops had schooled Jax in the proper way a man should treat a lady, serving as a role model in the myriad of ways that he had treated his grandmother and his mom special. Pops never let a woman open a door if he was around, or pull out a chair at a table, or do any heavy lifting. He held an umbrella over his ladies' heads if walking in the rain and offered his arm strolling a street. Pops even brought his wife and daughter flowers at least once a month just because. Pops revered mothers and women in general and he taught his grandson to do the same.

Sandra may have labeled Jax a momma's boy, but he didn't care. Sofia meant the world to fatherless Jax—even more so after Pops' death. And Jax had always treated Sandra or any woman he had dated just as old school. Much to Jax's chagrin, Brooke might not enjoy his chivalry.

Jax wiped off the table Brooke had just cleared and gave a nod to his mom to seat the next customers. Brooke barreled through the swinging door carrying another heavy tray loaded with full glasses of ice water. She zipped up to the front of the restaurant and offered drinks to the waiting customers. And then she brought water outside smiling and graciously welcoming people to his mom's place.

That done, she returned inside and waited on the table that Sofia had just seated.

This woman could train me.

She sure didn't need Jax to oversee her work, so he set to the task of handling the rush, glad that at least for that day, Sofia would be happy with the receipts tally.

An hour and a half later, the line had disappeared, all diners were fed, and a couple of tables of customers lingered sipping coffee and chatting. Brooke drifted up front to join Sofia, and Jax decided to spend some time doing paper work in the back office.

When he had finished that task an hour later, he emerged into the main dining room where he found his mother and Brooke sitting on stools behind the front counter, laughing and hanging over Sofia's cell phone.

"What's so funny?" He looked over Sofia's shoulder.

She had her photo app open, and she scrolled through old photos of him showing Brooke what a little dork he was as a kid—apparently much to Brooke's amusement.

"Now this one," Sofia said, "was taken at Disneyland."

"Uh huh. The Mickey Mouse ears," Brooke said.

"Right. He wouldn't take those darned things off for days. He was totally obsessed. The Mickey Mouse Club was his favorite thing."

Brooke shot him a grin. "Meeska Mooska…"

Jax narrowed his eyes at Brooke. "Good grief, Ma. Next thing you'll show her baby naked in the bathtub photos."

"You have those, Sofia?"

Sofia knit her brow in concentration fiddling with her phone. "Maybe…"

"Enough, mother."

"But we're having so much fun," Brooke said. "I really liked that six-shooter cowboy pic."

"Here's one of him with his buddies at college," Sofia said.

Brooke squinted at Sofia's phone. "Whoa. Handsome. Jax, your friends in this photo are hot."

He grinned. "And I'm…?"

She gave him a wry smile. "Hot, too and fishing for compliments."

"However I can get one," he said. "Are you hungry, Brooke? We can eat before you leave today."

"Famished." She stepped out from behind the counter. "Will you join us, Sofia?"

"I'm good." Sofia winked at her son. "You kids enjoy some alone time."

For once Jax didn't mind his mother's implied match making. Brooke walked with him to a back booth nearest the kitchen and took a seat.

"What would you like?" he said.

"Kind of addicted to the Pops' Special, please."

"Sure. Give me a sec."

He swung into the kitchen, gave Sergio his order and loaded the dishwasher while he waited for the cook to prepare their food.

Ten minutes later he brought their breakfasts over to the table and sat across from her.

She dug in to her eggs and bacon with relish while Jax enjoyed watching her eat, fixating on her lips as she chewed her food.

"So, how was your first day?"

"Good. I really enjoyed it, actually." She dabbed her lips with a napkin. "How do you think I did? I hope you want me back tomorrow."

"You did great, and I absolutely want you to continue working here. Frankly, I think my mother would kill me if I said otherwise."

Brooke beamed at him, her lovely face glowing. Jax thanked the fates for her lucky appearance and spontaneous job application the day before.

"Are you sure you don't want me to stay until closing? I can help you to serve tables and clean up."

"Thanks, but we'll be lucky if we have a table or two of customers. I'm seriously thinking about recommending that we close around noon every day and just serve breakfast if Mom will go along with the idea. She may not."

"Really, why?"

"Because Pops will probably roll over in his grave if I mess with the café's hours."

"Speaking of your grandfather, what did he think of Sofia's husband?"

Jax didn't like Pops' and Thurston Baxter's names included in the same sentence. "He couldn't stand the guy, but he never expressed his opinion to Mom because he knew how lonely she was when I left for college in Alabama. I, on the other hand, have never hidden my loathing for the guy."

"You didn't want your mother to remarry? Is that it?"

"Not at all. I'm all for her happiness. I just wish she had chosen a better life partner."

"I guess to each his own, right? Has your stepfather made any effort to improve your relationship with him?"

"Ha! Not at all. I want him to improve his relationship with my mother. I can't stand the way he treats her."

"He's not abusive, is he?"

"Not physically, if that's what you mean. I'd kill him if he ever laid a hand on her. He's emotionally abusive—cold as ice. It would be such a simple thing for him to support her financially with this restaurant. It means the world to her. He's wealthy and a workaholic at Mercury Labs so her hours here don't impact him at all. It would cost him very little to support her dreams for this place."

Sofia bustled over to their table. "How about you and your brother come to dinner at my house this evening? Jax, of course, you, too. I'm a very good cook, right Jax?"

The last thing he wanted was to spend any time in his stepfather's company. "You're a great cook, Ma. But dinner at your house is out for me."

"Aw, Jax," Sofia groused. "I thought maybe you'd reconsider if Brooke and Mike were included."

"Nice try, Ma." He gazed at Brooke. "You and Mike are welcome to go. Don't let me stop you."

She narrowed her eyes and gazed at him. "Thank

you, Sofia, but maybe another time. Mike started work this morning and he'll probably stay late to impress his new management."

Sofia frowned. "All right, honey. Consider it an open invitation."

"If you don't have anything else for me, I think I'll head home, Jax."

Jax nodded agreement and Brooke rose from the table. "Okay, boss. I'll see you in the morning. Thanks again for the job."

Chapter 6

Jax had surprised Brooke before she left work by inviting her to meet his friends at a bar for a couple of drinks that evening. An even bigger surprise was how genuinely excited she was at his invitation.

It looked like a bomb had exploded in Brooke's room. Jeans and shirts were strewn across her bed. Shoes were scattered on the floor. She couldn't remember the last time she had gone on a date, and she hadn't brought anything resembling a date outfit from home, anticipating only work during her stay in Luna Beach.

Brooke shoved aside the clothes, plopped down on the bed and buried her head in her hands.

"What happened?"

Brooke startled at Mike's booming voice.

He stood in the doorway wearing a shocked expression. "Are you hurt? Have we been robbed?"

"No nothing like that. I just can't find anything to wear."

"You're kidding me, right?" No mistaking the edge in his voice.

"I left my nicer clothes at home. I didn't expect to go out on a date." She rose from the bed and started to straighten up the mess.

"You do realize that you're not actually going on a date. Who cares what you wear?" he hollered. "Just do your job, Special Agent." Mike turned away and stomped down the hall.

"How dare you," she spat out.

Brooke followed him into his perfectly organized room. "You're not my father nor my boss on this Op. We're *partners* and you do not get to speak to me this way. I'm working just as hard as you are on this investigation."

She spun on her heel, returned to her room, slammed the door shut and blinked away angry tears. She would never admit it to Mike, but he was right. Jax had become more than a suspect. Brooke had real feelings for him and before Mike had forced her to weigh her actions, she had viewed the evening ahead as their first date.

The apartment door slammed. *Good. Leave me alone.*

Brooke straightened up her room and slipped on her dressiest jeans and a loose sweater. She gave her lashes a quick brush of mascara and applied lip gloss. More or less ready, she drifted into the main room, sat on the couch, powered on the TV and waited, hoping Mike would come back soon with the car.

An hour later Mike burst through the door carrying two bags.

"I'm sorry." He handed her one of the bags.

She peered inside at the pretty, pale yellow, crocheted top. "I don't understand."

"I called Kay to complain about you. To say she was mad at me is an understatement. I did as she asked, went to the mall and then video called her. She picked out that sweater for you to wear tonight."

"Wow. That's so nice of you. And her. Thank you."

"I really am sorry for yelling at you. I had a tough first day. My access at Mercury is strictly limited and we can't move as fast as I had hoped. But as Kay said, I had no right to take it out on you. I know you're a professional, Brooke, and you'll remain objective. I was out of line.

"And to prove I really do know you…" He dug inside the other bag and produced a large ice cream Blizzard.

"Is that vanilla with chocolate cookie crumbles?"

"You know it is." He gave her a crooked grin.

"And I'll bet there's a chocolate peanut butter cup Blizzard in there, too." She smiled at him.

"See, we do know each other." He took his cup out of the bag. "Forgive me?"

She hugged him in response and then dug into her treat, savoring every sip.

The sweater fit perfectly and Brooke texted Kay to thank her.

Kay responded,

—*I hope you're wearing it with those black jeans that make your ass look amazing. I told Mike to tell you that, but I have a feeling he didn't.*—

She ended the text with a laughing smiley face and a blowing a kiss emoji.

Brooke put a heart on Kay's text, missing her best friend and sister of the heart sorely. She decided that when her work was done here, she'd visit Kay before returning home.

Car keys in hand, Brooke faced Mike. "I won't be late. Tomorrow is a work day. And I *know* tonight is a work night."

"See you later." He slurped on his straw.

Peggy's Place, Brooke's destination, was a couple of towns away from Luna Beach. Following the Waze

Ap had her avoiding the traffic on the coast highway. She pulled into the bar's parking lot. Her pulse raced at the sight of Jax leaning against the lot's perimeter wall.

This is my job, not a date. This is my job, not a date. Brooke repeated the mantra in her mind as she parked the car and slipped out of the driver's seat.

Jax walked over to her.

Damn, he looks good.

His reddish-brown hair curled slightly behind his ears, tempting her to thread her fingers through the softness. He wore an untucked, crisp white dress shirt with the sleeves rolled up on his muscular forearms. Her mantra dissolved the moment he smiled.

She walked by his side toward the entrance. "Sorry I'm late. I had to wait for Mike to get back with the car."

"No problem. Hunter and Lyndsey are inside holding a table for us." Jax opened the door for her.

He clasped her hand, led her past the bar, and across a dance floor where a mountain of a man, who had to be Hunter, stood waving them to their table.

"Hunter and Lyndsey, this is Brooke," Jax said.

First Lyndsey and then Hunter enveloped Brooke in an embrace.

"We're huggers. I hope you don't mind," Lyndsey said.

"I don't mind at all. I'm a hugger, too." Brooke smiled at the couple.

Jax pulled out a chair for Brooke and the foursome took seats at the table.

A waitress supplied a pitcher of beer.

"Can I please have a Diet Coke when you get a chance?" Brooke said.

"I'm sorry. I should have asked you what you want

to drink." Jax leaned towards her. His cologne was woodsy with a hint of lemon.

How could one man be so delicious? He was so close that if she turned her head, their lips might meet. She resisted testing that hypothesis, eyes forward on Lyndsey and Hunter.

"It's so nice to meet you both. Have you and Jax been friends for a long time?"

"Oh man. Jax and I have been friends since middle school when we were both on the junior high baseball team. I'm a year older," Hunter said, "and I'll never forget the day Jax made the team. I'm a catcher and here comes this skinny quiet kid who said to the coach that he's a pitcher. Coach is like, show me your stuff and tells me to catch for him. Jax threw the fastest and hardest ball I ever caught, and he made the team that day. We've been best friends ever since."

"I met Jax senior year when my family moved to town. We were in the same classes," Lyndsey chimed in. "I didn't get to know Hunter until a few years later."

"How did you meet Hunter?"

Jax guffawed. "Yeah, Hunter how *did* you guys meet?"

Hunter narrowed his eyes at Jax. "Okay, maybe it wasn't my finest moment."

He gazed at Lyndsey, his face alight, his eyes tender. "But it was the best moment of my life."

Lyndsey beamed at him, the love between them palpable. "Aw, Hunter. Mine, too. Although, I didn't think that way at first. I was driving home. A pickup truck was stopped on the side of the road with a flat rear tire. So I pulled over to see if I could help. A big lug of a man was trying to figure out how to change the tire. So

I changed the tire for him." She took a big sip of her beer.

"It was the sexiest thing I ever saw in my life. I've been hooked ever since," Hunter said.

"Hunter didn't know it then, but my dad owns a gas and service center, and I've been working on cars my whole life. I wish you could have seen his face when I popped that wheel off; just priceless."

A group of men at the table behind Jax and Hunter captured Brooke's attention. Their loud laughter and unruly behavior magnified as they drained pitchers of beer as fast as the waitress supplied them.

Brooke kept an eye on them. "This is such a nice place. It has an Irish pub feel to it."

"You'll have to tell that to Peggy when you meet her." Jax put his arm around the back of Brooke's chair.

"There really is a Peggy? And you know her? When would I ever meet her?"

A tall, elegant, red-haired woman closed in on the table. She wrapped her arms around Hunter from behind and kissed the top of his head.

"Hi, Mom," Hunter said.

"It's so good to see my boys," she said.

"I was about to tell you that Peggy, who is Hunter's mom, was on her way to our table," Jax whispered in Brooke's ear.

Peggy gave Lyndsey a hug and then skirted the table toward Jax. "I haven't seen you in way too long. How's Mom doing?"

Jax stood and hugged Peggy. "She's good. Thanks for visiting her at the hospital. It meant the world to her."

"You know I love her and if she needs anything you tell her to call me. I'm so glad you came home to be with her. How long are you staying?"

"A couple more weeks at least, until I know she's back on her feet."

"Is anyone going to introduce me to this beautiful young woman? Did you bring her with you from New York?" She offered her hand to Brooke.

"Peggy this is Brooke James. Brooke is working for my mom now. She just moved here from the east coast."

Brooke accepted the handshake. "It's lovely to meet you, Peggy. I was just telling Jax that your bar reminds me of an Irish pub."

"I'm so glad you noticed. It's intentional. A nod to my family's roots. I hope to see you again soon. Now I'm heading home. You boys behave yourselves." She patted her "boys" on their shoulders and stepped away.

"Do you work here with your mom, Hunter?"

"No. I work with my dad. He owns a commercial real estate company."

"And Hunter is about to be a published author. I'm so proud of him," Lyndsey said.

"Really? Congratulations. What's your genre?"

"Sports Fiction Suspense. The book launch is next month."

"That sounds right up my alley. I love to read. I'll be first in line to buy an autographed copy." *Although I hope I'm not here next month.*

The noise level from the drunken bunch nearby elevated, nearly drowning out the conversation at Brooke's table.

"We've been going on and on about us, but we don't know anything about you, Brooke. Were you a waitress on the east coast?" Lyndsey said.

"No." Brooke's thoughts scrambled as she worked to concoct a cover. She landed on the quasi-truth. "I worked in a large chain bookstore. It was perfect for me. As I said, I love to read."

"What an awesome job. All those books surrounding you. I love to read, too, so I think I would spend every penny of my paycheck buying them."

"Luckily, I got a sweet employee discount." She did spend most of her minimum wage pay from the part-time job at the bookstore when she was in high school.

A voice from the boisterous table boomed. "Things will get nasty if you don't bring us another pitcher," one guy said.

Lanyards hung around their necks. Brooke figured that they were partying away from home at a business conference. The men were arguing with the waitress who apparently wanted to cut them off.

"I'll be right back." Brooke pushed her chair away from the table and rose to her feet.

Jax and Hunter turned around in their seats, their gazes following Brooke's strides toward the table behind them.

"Good evening, gentlemen." Six heads snapped in Brooke's direction. "Your waitress is just doing her job. From what I heard, I'm assuming she told you that you're overserved."

"Yes, she did and that is *bullshit*. If we want another pitcher of beer she can't tell us we can't have it," the guy who had threatened the waitress said.

"You're wrong. The bar has every right to tell you that you have had enough." Brooke kept her voice soft, pleasant. "I have a deal for you. I challenge you to a chugging contest. One round only. If any of you win, I'll pay your bar tab. But if I win, you'll call it a night, pay your tab, over-tip your waitress, and head back to your hotel. Deal?"

"Yeah, sure. Why not? You have a deal," the apparent ring leader said.

"I'll be right with you." Brooke stepped over to the bar for a pitcher of beer and an empty glass.

Back at their table, Brooke filled all of the glasses except for one of the men who opted out of the contest to conduct a count down. On the count of three the beer chugging began. Brooke slammed her glass down on the table a full five seconds before the first man finished chugging his beer.

"Thank you, gentlemen. Enjoy the rest of your conference."

Brooke returned to her seat next to Jax and took a delicate sip of her Diet Coke. Hunter's mouth hung open and Jax just stared at her.

"That was so hot. Jax, if you don't marry her I will."

Lyndsey elbowed Hunter in the side. "Hello. Your wife is sitting right next to you." She burst out laughing. "Men are so easy. But damn girl where did you ever learn to chug beer like that? I don't think I saw you swallow once."

"Let's just say that I never had to pay for a beer when I was in college."

The waitress came over to their table with their bill after the men had left. She thanked Brooke for her help. Hunter took out his credit card and paid for their drinks. Jax tried to hand his card to her, too, but Hunter waved him away. Jax put cash on the table to take care of the tip.

Hunter, Lyndsey, Jax and Brooke walked out to the parking lot together.

"It was really great to meet you, Brooke." Lyndsey

gave her a hug. "We're having our summer beach barbeque on Sunday. We'd love it if you both could come."

"I wouldn't miss it," Jax said. "Will you come with me, Brooke?"

This is my job. It is not a second date. "I'd love to."

"Perfect. We'll see you both on Sunday." Hunter put his arm around Lyndsey, and they walked towards the back of the lot.

Jax ushered Brooke to her car. "I could pick you up for the barbeque so your brother could have the car."

"That would be great. Thanks."

"Do you two only own one car?"

"Actually, we rented only one car. We sold our cars before we moved. It was so expensive to ship them coast to coast. We figured we'd go car shopping once we're more settled." The lies mounted.

"Makes sense," Jax said.

"Thank you for such a great night. I really like your friends." Brooke unlocked the car door and turned right into Jax's broad chest.

He dipped his head and brushed a kiss over her lips, leaving her legs wobbly. On sheer impulse, Brooke encircled her arms around his waist and kissed him. He deepened the kiss, drawing her close.

She melted in his arms. *This is a job not a date.* Her mantra flashed in her mind tearing her away from his embrace.

"Wow," she whispered.

"Wow," he echoed.

"I'll see you in the morning." She opened her car door and slipped inside as fast as she could. With a quick wave she drove out of the parking lot.

In her rearview mirror Jax watched her drive away. *This was not a date. This is a job.*

Chapter 7

From Tuesday through Sunday that week, Brooke focused on excelling at her waitressing job and looking for opportunities to question her suspects without their questioning her true intent.

The regulars had grown on her and warmed Brooke's heart, especially Lily Levant. She had become fond of the thorny old lady and apparently the feeling was mutual. Lily went so far as to propose including Brooke in her will as the granddaughter she wished she had and cutting out her "supremely disappointing" grandson. Brooke had kissed Lily on her soft cheek and gently rejected the notion.

The group that she had dubbed Donald and the Four in her mind insisted on overtipping her every day. They were vocal about that fact emphasizing what a big deal it was since they were all on "fixed incomes."

Even the wayward group leader who thought his hand belonged on her rear end had seen the error of his ways. He, too, overtipped and pointedly sat on his hands grinning at her whenever she served their table.

She offered to help Jax make entries into the books for Pops' Café during the lull between breakfast and lunch. He took her up on the offer seemingly out of the goodness of his heart misinterpreting her willingness to do the administrative work as her way to make a few extra dollars. His accounting system was simple and meticulous. The ledger only proved that Sofia wasn't tapping her multi-million-dollar bank account to inject money into her restaurant. Were it not for the monthly supplements from Jax, the business would certainly shutter.

Following the money would involve delving into Jax's and Sofia's personal finances. That information would likely reside in their homes: check books, bank statements and online banking accounts. She mentally kicked herself that she hadn't figured out a way to accept Sofia's recent dinner invitation despite Jax's strong objection. Getting inside the Baxter mansion might have provided a chance to snoop around. Although if Thurston Baxter were home, maybe not.

Mike made slow progress at Mercury Labs. Both he and Brooke were driven to obtain airtight evidence to convict the traitors. It wasn't falling in their laps. But they were trained to conduct methodical investigations and patience was critical. Brooke's patience was thin. A quick wrap up of the Op in Luna Beach grew more imperative.

She had to leave as soon as possible. Because if she didn't, she feared she'd never want to let Jax go. Despite her mantra and resolve to remain impersonal and unentangled with a suspect, her heart betrayed her. Believing that Jax was innocent of the crimes his family was committing, Brooke couldn't decide if her feelings for Jax clouded that judgment or not. Mike, or God forbid her father, could never know that her law enforcer objectivity disintegrated in the light of his smile or the touch of his hand—not to mention the heat of his kiss.

Brooke passed on joining Jax for a late breakfast before leaving the restaurant on Sunday explaining that she had errands to run to the grocery and bakery stores to bring something to the beach barbeque that evening. Jax reextended his offer to pick her up at the apartment, but she had other ideas. She asked for his address and told him she'd meet him there. Brooke dutifully entered the personal information that he recited into her phone, even though she had memorized where he lived and a lot more from the case file. His nearness had her dizzy with desire—totally the opposite of how she should relate to him.

Even so, she breezed out of the restaurant looking forward to that evening and spending as much time with him as possible before the investigation was over. She stopped at a convenience store situated midway between her apartment and the café where she bought brownies, donuts and a couple bags of chips—hardly bakery fare, but she figured presentable enough to contribute to the party.

Back in her cell block bedroom she changed her clothes. Choosing what to wear for that "not a date, but the job" was easy—shorts with zipper pockets, sandals, a soft, powder blue, cotton tunic and a hoody for a cooler evening by the ocean. She wound her long mane into a chignon and pinned it at the nape of her neck. Her cell phone fit into the right pocket of her shorts. She stowed her keys and a flash drive memory stick in the left pocket and zipped both pockets closed.

Brooke hung over the open refrigerator door scrounging for something to eat for lunch. Unflavored Greek yogurt was her only option. Brooke spooned some into her mouth and grimaced at the sourness. "Yuck, Mike, and your rabid health consciousness."

Brooke sat at the counter with her better-than-going-hungry meal and thumbed through the magazine that she had picked up at the convenience store. Her cell phone vibrated against her thigh, and she took it out of her pocket. A quick glance at the screen had her straightening her spine and rapidly sliding a finger across the bottom of the readout to answer her father's call.

"Good afternoon, sir."

"Progress report, Special Agent."

"I plan to surveille Jaxon Rosso's residence this evening."

"Promising. Should I bring in a TacOps team to plant electronic surveillance at this juncture?"

"No sir. I think that's premature, and I'm not convinced yet that Jax would reveal anything useful. From questioning him the past week, I doubt his involvement. But of course…" she hurried to add, "I won't draw any solid conclusions this early in the investigation."

"Good. Talk soon."

White noise in her ear. She sighed and returned to paging through the magazine.

Bored with reading about celebrity summer vacations and personal traumas, she rose from the stool, tossed the empty yogurt container in the trash and headed back to her bedroom. She stretched out on the bed and read a romance novel straight to the happily ever after until it was time to leave.

The novel's emotional ending after the up and down dance between the heroine and hero brought tears to her eyes. Fictional characters could overcome conflicts and find true love. Brooke wished that an HEA was possible in real life…for her…with Jax.

No point to wishing.

Brooke carried her contribution to the barbecue in a shopping bag while strolling the four blocks to Jax's condo. She arrived early at his doorstep on purpose. He answered her doorbell ring wearing only a towel, his brown hair shower-slicked black and his defined pecs and abs on glorious display.

"I'm so sorry," she lied. "Am I early?"

His broad smile stoked her desire, but she reined in her impulses and focused on the purpose of her early arrival. She was delighted to find his open laptop on the gleaming marble kitchen counter when Jax ushered her inside the pristine condo. Decorated in earth tones with modern leather furniture and abstract paintings on the walls, his place projected casual elegance. She wondered if his grandparents or Jax were the interior decorators.

"Make yourself at home, Brooke. I just need to finish sending a quick email."

He stood at the counter, typed a couple strokes on the keyboard and then a whoosh sounded. Brooke enjoyed the view of his sculpted back muscles and the drape of the towel over his rear end.

"I'll shave and get dressed. Help yourself to anything in the fridge. I'll be back in a few minutes."

Brooke watched him retreat down the hall before taking a seat on a stool at the counter in front of his computer. She hit a key to bring the display alive and smiled when she saw that the laptop had yet to go into lock mode. She plugged in her portable flash drive and transferred all the pertinent files, pocketing the memory stick. Brooke figured that Mike could work his magic to analyze the data.

She couldn't resist opening his photo app while she waited for Jax. Brooke bit back jealousy, encountering the beautiful images of him with a woman. She had no business looking at the happy couple and surely had no right to be jealous. But she was. Brooke closed the Ap and drifted over to the wall of windows facing the sea.

The gorgeous view soothed and grounded her. Spending time with Jax blotted out the truth of her mission. Brooke had never cared for a man the way that she cared about Jax. Was it selfish to want him? She had to admit it was. But the attraction was too strong for her to ignore.

She felt him come up behind her, but she didn't turn around. Jax put his arms around her, and she leaned back against his chest thrilling at the rightness of resting in his embrace. His warm breath tickled her ear. "Ready?"

His sensual magnetism had her swoony. She turned around within the circle of his arms and beamed up at him. "Yes, I'm ready." *To jump straight into your bed.* "Is it walking distance on the beach?" She moved toward the door needing to escape the intimacy of his home before she did something she'd regret.

"No, too far to walk. But it's a short drive." He grabbed car keys out of a ceramic bowl on the counter and then opened a door off the kitchen. "After you."

Brooke stepped into the garage blinking in the sunlight as the door raised. Jax opened the passenger door of a sleek, black two-seater, rag top convertible. She eased into the low seat inhaling the rich, new car smell. Jax sat behind the wheel and engaged the mechanism to detract the convertible top. He reversed out of the garage, down the driveway, shifted into gear and zoomed onto the coast highway.

Tendrils from her chignon loosened by the wind brushed against her face in the rushing open air. The warm sunshine, the briny scent of the sea and the glorious views exhilarated her. Brooke felt light and free and capable of ignoring her real reason for being with Jax. For that evening she'd just enjoy the company of a sexy man and his nice friends.

Hunter, apparently always the athlete, had organized a sand volleyball game on the beach. Jax immediately opted to join Hunter's team. "Want to play, Brooke?"

"I do, but I'm going to see if I can help Lyndsey with anything first."

Jax ambled to Hunter's side of the net. Brooke took off her sandals and slogged through the sand over to Lyndsey and a group of people congregating around a firepit. Beach blankets were spread out near the pit where flames took hold of kindling and spread to pieces of wood.

"Hi Brooke," Lyndsey said. "Guys, this is Brooke, Jax's girlfriend. Brooke, this is Carol—married to Bob, Sally—married to John, Deb married to Wayne, Kathy married to Paul and Mavis married to Nick All the men are playing volleyball with Hunter and Jax right now."

Hi's and little waves followed each introduction, so Brooke was able to connect the names of the women with faces. She'd have no trouble calling them by name for the rest of the evening.

Brooke handed Lyndsey her shopping bag. "Brownies, donuts and chips," she said.

"Thanks. This is perfect." Lyndsey emptied the bag and placed the contents out on a card table. "We're not fancy with the menu. We have five long sub sandwiches and plenty of hot dogs to grill over the fire with packages of buns and condiments.

"There are beers, sodas and bottled water in those

coolers over there." Lyndsey pointed to a spot on a blanket under an umbrella. "And, of course, marshmallows to roast and fixings for smores."

"Sounds great. What can I do to help?"

"Not a thing. Go play with the boys or get to know my friends. You'll love them and I know they'll love you."

Brooke plopped down on an unoccupied blanket situated between Deb and Mavis. "Mind if I join you?"

"Not at all. Welcome." Mavis held out a can in each hand. "Care for a ginger ale or a beer?"

"Ginger ale, please."

She handed Brooke the soda.

"If I start drinking beer now I'll be looped by dinner time."

"I'm with you there," Deb said. "Lyndsey tells us you moved here from Virginia. How do you like living in SoCal?"

"What's not to like." Brooke smiled. "The weather is flat out gorgeous, and I could gaze at the ocean for days and never get bored." *Too bad I don't really live here.*

"Right?" Mavis wrapped her arms around her bent knees. "I love to walk the beach in the mornings. It's so peaceful. Plus if I didn't have the seaside to enjoy, I'd probably never exercise at all!"

"Oh and the sunsets," Brooke added. "I caught one the other night and it was spectacular."

"See those scattered clouds on the horizon?" Deb said.

"Uh huh."

"They'll make for a really pretty sunset tonight."

"I'll probably take a million photos," Brooke said.

Her newfound friends nodded and smiled and then resumed gazing at the waves. Brooke did, too, feeling relaxed and free to simply enjoy every moment of the get together.

She lost track of time hypnotized by the undulating waves and the play of sunlight on the glassy water. Beyond the breakers, Brooke spied dolphin fins curving above the surface and then disappearing. One dolphin jumped straight up in the air and then nose-dived back into the water. Deb, Mavis and Brooke gasped in unison.

The men stampeded over to their spot on the beach stirring up the sand nearby and smelling of sweat. Jax walked over to Brooke, a beer can in hand. He guzzled down the drink and squeezed the can flat within his fist.

"Want to go for a swim?"

"I didn't bring a suit, and I don't want to sit in wet clothes all night," she said.

He waggled his eyebrows. "I have a solution…"

She laughed at the implication. "Nah—skinny dipping—especially around a crowd—isn't my style."

"Darn." He whipped his POLO shirt over his head, took off his shoes and socks and tossed them on Brooke's blanket.

And then he headed straight for the water on the run along with the pack of volleyball players.

When Jax joined her on the blanket after drying himself off with the beach towel that Lyndsey provided and shrugging into a sweat shirt, the fire's flames danced in the pit and the sky's color mimicked the flames. Jax wrapped his arm around her, and she leaned her head against his shoulder, his shirt's material soft against her cheek and smelling of his enticing aftershave.

Chapter 8

Hunter and Lyndsey gathered up picnic remnants with Mavis and Nick after the other four couples at the beach barbecue went home.

"Let's go help with clean up," Brooke said.

"Sure." Jax grabbed Brooke's hand and hauled her to her feet off the blanket.

"Everything was delicious." Brooke carried the tray of leftover s'mores fixings, walking at Lyndsey's side.

"Thanks. But it was nothing special. You don't have to be Gordon Ramsey to cook hot dogs," Lyndsey said. "But you'll have to come to our Christmas party this year. I have it catered, and the food is divine."

A lump formed in Brooke's throat. If only she were really Jax's girlfriend. They could plan the holidays together. She could enjoy a true friendship with Lyndsey and take her up on her invitation.

Brooke followed Lyndsey through the sliding glass door into her beachfront home. In the gleaming kitchen, so unlike the ugly excuse for the same room in her apartment, Brooke set her tray down on an oval table, nabbed a square of chocolate and popped it in her mouth. Two gray French bulldogs barreled across the room towards her.

"Oh my goodness." Brooke squatted down. She barely kept her balance when the wiggly, chubby pups leaped on her.

"Mabel and Millie, down please!" Lyndsey's command had no effect on Mabel and Millie.

Brooke sat down on the tile floor and let the dogs jump all over her.

"I'm in love." She lavished Millie and Mabel with petting and belly rubbing. "I so wanted a dog growing up. But my dad was allergic." *Or was he?*

"Have to admit, these little ones have stolen my heart. Who's hungry?"

Brooke hooted at Mabel's and Millie's instant abandonment. The pups skittered over to their food bowls.

Jax lugged a cooler inside and deposited it on the kitchen floor next to the center island.

Brooke rose from the floor to stand by Jax's side. He casually hung his left arm around her shoulders cocooning her in his tantalizing warmth.

"Great seeing you, Jax," Nick shook Jax's hand. "Hunter tells me your mom is doing well now."

"She is. Thank God."

"Does that mean you'll head back to the big city soon?" Mavis said.

"I guess so."

"We'll miss you, but you'll come back for the Christmas party, right?"

"Wouldn't miss it." He gave Mavis a hug.

"Something tells me that you might come home more often now." Mavis smiled and winked at Brooke.

"Night everybody." Mavis and Nick left, bound for home.

"The sun hasn't completely set yet. Want to go back out to the beach?" Jax said.

She nodded and slipped her phone out of her pocket,

camera at the ready.

Repositioned on the beach blanket with Jax's comforting arm around her, Brooke stared at the sky that blazed gloriously with the sun's descent below the horizon. She was swamped by misgivings and didn't take a single photo.

What am I doing mingling with these couples adding to the nice people I'm deceiving?

Brooke had never before regretted fully committing to an undercover role. *But now?*

She genuinely liked Jax's friends, and it seemed that they liked her, too. Her fondness for those people and her deep feelings for Jax warred with a guilty conscience. As soon as she and Mike gathered the crucial evidence to prosecute Jax and his family they would disappear with no explanation. She'd have no contact with Jax, romantic or otherwise.

That was the job. For the first time in her career, she didn't like her job at all.

"You're awfully quiet. Is everything all right?"

Nothing is right about how I'm going to hurt you…and myself in the process.

She scooted closer to him until their hips touched. "I'm good. But I guess that I feel homesick after hearing you say you'll go home to New York soon. I'm kind of second guessing my decision to drop everything and move with my brother."

"Oh." He gave her a lopsided grin, his handsome face haloed by the sunset. "I thought maybe hearing about my leaving might make you miss me."

Her heart flipflopped. Soon, she'd lose what they had together and secretly she'd miss him sorely. "I'm so happy I met you, Jax. Of course I'll miss you. I don't want you to leave me."

At least that was the truth, although turned around. Brooke didn't want to leave Jax.

"You know, if you did move back to Virginia, it's three hundred and thirty miles from my condo in New York to the Chesapeake Bay Bridge Tunnel—less than six hours by car."

Her mind whirled. Could she possibly have her fantasy future with him despite her subterfuge? She knew in her heart that he wasn't a traitor. But how would he view her exposing his beloved mother? Brooke couldn't afford to get her hopes up that he could forgive her if his mother wound up behind bars.

"Why did you look up the driving distance to Virginia?"

His penetrating gaze locked on her eyes. "Why do you think?"

She wasn't alone in her feelings. Jax had begun to think long term, too.

"That's the sexiest thing I ever—"

He cut off her sentence with the gentlest kiss that she didn't want to end.

When he softly withdrew his lips, he said, "I'm thankful that you and your brother walked into Pops' place."

"Me too." She laid her head on his shoulder.

"What's your favorite ice cream flavor?" Jax said.

She lifted her head and knit her brows, gazing at him. "Where did that come from?"

"I want to know everything about you."

"Oh. Okay. I'm game. Black cherry. With chocolate cookie crumbles on top. What's yours?"

"I'd have to go with macadamia fudge coconut. I

had it once in Hawaii and I've never forgotten it."

"My turn." She faced him, folding her legs into the lotus position. "What's your favorite movie?"

"I'll go with *Field of Dreams*."

"That's a good one. I was afraid you were going to say anything Marvel."

"No. I'm more of a sports guy. What's yours?"

"I love musicals. *The Greatest Showman* is my all-time favorite. Kay and I have watched it countless times. We took a girls' trip to Palm Springs during spring break one year and we watched that movie every night."

"Who's Kay?"

"Oh, wow, I haven't mentioned her before? She's Mike's fiancée. I'm very close to her. Kay lived in the house next door to us growing up. I was thirteen and Mike was eighteen when our parents died. Mike received a full scholarship to MIT but was going to turn it down and stay home to take care of me. Kay's parents wouldn't hear of it. Kay's dad is a lawyer, and he petitioned the court for guardianship of me. I lived at Kay's house until Mike finished his degree. They're the kindest people. Kay and I are sisters in every meaning of the word. Those were some of the happiest years of my life."

She heaped lie upon lie, relaying her fictitious life story. Although she *did* practically live with Kay's family after her mother died. But she was only three at the time, not thirteen and there was no older brother Mike volunteering to take care of her. Her father didn't know how to deal with his grief or a toddler girl. He immersed himself in his job and hired people to raise her until Brooke entered kindergarten. Kay's mom volunteered to watch her before and after school and during summer vacations. The years Kay's mom took care of her *were* the happiest years of her life.

"Enough about me. When were you happiest in your life?"

"I'd have to say my time at college. Hunter and I both went to the University of Alabama because of baseball. I was recruited by a couple of great schools but when Alabama became interested in me, I decided to follow Hunter to the Crimson Tide. It was everything I hoped for and more. Being on the baseball team was a fantastic experience. We were unstoppable. We went undefeated and won the National Championship. *Sports Illustrated* dubbed us the Bama Boys in their feature article about the team and the championship game. We're all still close this many years since graduation. Like Kay is your sister, the Bama Boys are my brothers.

"How about your favorite pizza topping?" His question brought a smile to her face. Pizza was her favorite food.

"Sausage. What's yours?"

"Mushroom."

"Yuck. That's a deal breaker. Tastes like moldy dirt." Brooke stood up and brushed sand off her legs. "I feel like taking a run before it gets dark." She took off towards the water.

He chased her to the water's edge.

****

Jax caught up with Brooke and swept her off her feet into a fireman's carry. Holding her close in his arms, he never wanted to let her go.

"Put me down you mushroom lover." She wriggled in his arms.

"Careful. I could drop you in the water." He inched up to his calves in the gentle waves.

"You wouldn't dare." She clung to his neck.

He cradled her close to his chest, waded out of the water and carried her back to the blanket. Jax knelt on the soft cloth and eased into a sitting position so that Brooke sat in his lap.

She straddled him, cupped his face with her hands and drew him into a kiss. Her lips tasted like chocolate and honey. Her tongue slowly circled his mouth. Jax groaned with mounting need. He stroked his hands down her back, cupped her bottom and pulled her tight against his aroused body. His heart pounded in his chest.

"Millie and Mabel, come back here this instant!" Hunter shouted out.

Two furry bowling balls hurtled onto the blanket separating Brooke and Jax. Brooke doubled over laughing. Jax had to laugh, too.

Hunter caught his breath after catching up with the escape artists. "I'm sorry to bother you guys. I left my phone out on the deck. They slipped right past me the minute I slid open the door to go get the phone."

"I love them." Brooke snuggled Mabel in her lap.

Jax scowled at his friend but didn't stop rubbing Millie's belly. "No problem."

"Let's go home, girls." Hunter clapped his hands and reversed direction toward the house.

The "girls" stayed put.

"Who wants cheese?" Hunter called out still in motion.

Mabel and Millie froze in place. And then they torpedoed off the blanket racing after Hunter.

"Did we just get dumped for a piece of cheese?" Jax said.

"We certainly did. They're so cute, though."

"Well…" Jax left it there.

He stood up and held his hand out to Brooke. "It's getting dark, and we both have early wakeups. We should call it a night."

She placed her soft hand in his accepting his tow up. Each of them took a side of the blanket and shook off sand. Brooke folded it, draped it over her arm and walked with him to his car holding his hand.

"That was a fun evening." Brooke fiddled with the radio knob in the car until country music played on his excellent sound system.

"It *was* fun until the little beasts interrupted us." Jax reached sideways, clasped her hand and held it on top of his thigh.

"It's probably a good thing they interrupted us when they did. It would have been pretty embarrassing to be arrested for indecent exposure." She sang along with Kenny Chesney.

The arrest would have been worth it. "You like country music?"

"Love it. Do you?"

"I do. Another thing we have in common."

When he parked his car in front of her place, Jax didn't want to let go of her hand.

She leaned over and kissed him on the cheek. "Thanks for a wonderful night. See you in the morning, boss."

Brooke sprang out of the car and bounded up the flight of steps leading to her apartment. She blew him a kiss, used her key and opened the door. He watched the door close behind her and then pulled away, smiling all the way home.

After a quick hot shower, he grabbed a handful of

chocolate sandwich cookies from the glass jar on the kitchen counter, poured a mug of milk and strolled out to the deck. Popping a cookie into his mouth, he sat down on a cushioned, Adirondack chair and propped his bare feet up on the railing.

Closing his eyes he recalled the times he had sat in that exact spot with Pops. How he missed him and their ritual of enjoying cookies and milk while they star gazed. Pops had pointed out Orion's belt to him as the easiest way to find the constellation. No matter where he was since then, when he looked up at the night sky he'd search for Orion. When he singled out the constellation, he'd think of Pops and say hello.

Pops was the person Jax had always sought out for advice. He was a quiet, thoughtful man. His grandmother used to call him a man of few words. He once told Jax that the first time he saw Nana at a friend's wedding he knew she was the one for him. He was gob smacked. When Jax brought his dates around to meet him, Pops never said a word but gave a thumbs up or thumbs down behind her back. Jax laughed out loud at the memory.

Pops was a tough man, but Jax knew that he only wanted what was best for his grandson. Pops had convinced him to forget the other schools that courted him in high school and follow Hunter to Alabama. That was the best decision of Jax's life. Hiring Brooke might beat that decision as his all-time best.

What would Pops think of Brooke? Thumbs up or thumbs down?

He chugged the rest of the milk and stood up. Jax gripped the deck railing and looked up at the sky. He smiled at Orion. "Hey Pops."

A shooting star blazed across the sky above the

constellation.

"I knew you would like her, Pops. I'm gob smacked."

Chapter 9

Mike was asleep when Brooke arrived home, so she couldn't give him her prize flash drive stick that night. She was disappointed with the delay but from a personal perspective, maybe not. Mike didn't miss body language cues, and she was downright moony walking into her crummy apartment after the evening with Jax, her earlier subterfuge doing her job forgotten in his sexy thrall.

Brooke kicked off her sandals, plucked them up from the floor in one hand and padded barefoot to her room after depositing the drive on the kitchen counter with a quick note to her partner explaining its contents. She hoped that whatever evidence she had gleaned by stealing data from Jax's laptop would exonerate rather than implicate him.

What would it mean for her if he were proven innocent? Could they have a future together? The hardworking finance guy and the duplicitous FBI Agent who would probably lock up his mother and stepfather in a Federal penitentiary for life? Jax wouldn't shed a single tear over Thurston Baxter's probable fate. But Sofia? She had no doubt that if Sofia wound up in jail when their investigation concluded, Jax would want nothing to do with Brooke—ever.

That likelihood didn't stop Brooke from dreaming a different outcome. In her slumber, cute little dogs hadn't stopped their prelude to lovemaking on the beach blanket under the night sky. Their first union was perfect, cosmic, just like the stars and planets that glittered above them.

She dreamed that Jax and Sofia were both innocent. When she and Mike locked his stepfather up, Jax was thrilled that his mom was free from the ogre's grasp. Her lies only mattered to him for a heartbeat. He was indebted to her and patiently listened to every word as she revealed her true identity. Dreamscape Jax thought that her law enforcer job was admirable, kick ass—sexy. He wanted forever with Special Agent Brooke Pellington, the nation's FBI Director's only child, forgiving her for using her mother's maiden name and lying that Mike was her sibling.

But even in her dreams, Brooke knew that she deceived herself in fantasy just as much as she deceived Jax in reality. She woke up to the harp tones of her cell phone's alarm with tears on her cheeks.

In the shower, she washed away the tears and steeled herself to continue to play her role and to ferret out the truth while secretly enjoying Jax's company for as long as the investigation took. Maybe, just maybe if only Thurston Baxter was proven a traitor, Jax might forgive her in time. It was a slim hope, but she clung to it anyway. She couldn't let on to her partner or her by-the-book father that despite her professional training, she had fallen in love with a prime suspect.

Brooke tiptoed out of the apartment at 5:15 a.m., forty-five minutes before sunrise. She tapped on her cell phone's flashlight to navigate on foot to Pops' Café. Brooke had come to love the quiet walk to work in the shadows, the early start time and the motley crew of regulars during the breakfast hours. Jax's nearness and her growing attraction to him added an extra dose of happiness to her days despite her conflicted emotions. She wanted the investigation to end so that she could return to her real life on the opposite coast just as much as she never wanted it to end so that she could stay there with Jax.

She expertly handled the crowd and the customers' demands side by side with Jax until the late morning lull. When he disappeared into the office to do paperwork, as was his daily habit, she brought a coffee for herself and a cappuccino for Sofia up to the front counter.

"Ooh, thank you." Sofia took a sip of her drink and smiled. "So good. I love Sergio's cappuccinos."

Brooke took a seat on the stool next to the café owner. "I made the espresso drink for you, Sofia. Glad you like it."

"A barista, too? We sure hit the jackpot hiring you, girl."

The praise warmed Brooke's guilty heart. At least she did a good job for Sofia and Jax while she and Mike worked toward blasting their world apart.

She took a sip from her mug, casual, just the hired help taking a break with the big boss. "So, I love to hear people's love stories. How did you and your husband meet? Was he a customer here?"

Sofia barked a laugh. "Hell no. Thurston is not a pancakes and eggs kind of guy. Strictly microgreens and power shakes for breakfast every day before dawn and then straight to the office. I met him before my father died. At the office. I was his technology assistant at Mercury Labs. Just for a month. He didn't want me to work once we were married, and he proposed on our second date. Our third date was a trip to Las Vegas. We got married in a wedding chapel there. So romantic."

How had the Bureau missed that Sofia and Baxter had worked together? Was Sofia the criminal mastermind? That would explain her fat bank account. And who better to transmit files to the Chinese than an assistant sitting at a computer all day. Did she or Thurston expunge her employee file? Somebody must have.

"That sounds like a fairy tale love story. So your husband doesn't want you to work? Why?"

"Oh…" She sipped from her cup. "He thought it wasn't appropriate for a boss and a subordinate who were married to work at the same company and he's old fashioned. He makes a big salary, and I guess he doesn't want people to think that he can't provide for his wife. After Dad died and I took over here, he was not happy with me, to say the least."

"No? Then why don't you hire a manager or maybe even sell the restaurant?"

Sofia wagged her head. "No way. I feel like I would be betraying my sweet father if I let this place go. And it may be stupid, but as long as Pops' Café exists, my dad lives on. I miss him so much."

"I can understand that. Is your husband's opposition to your working here the reason why Jax doesn't…um…"

"Why my son can't stand my husband? Yes. That's a big factor. Plus he feels like my loneliness when he was away at college was the reason I rushed into marriage with Thurston."

"I kind of gathered that. Does that make things difficult for you?"

"Well, it's sure not ideal. But Jax is a grown man

who has his own life in New York. I learned long ago that I can't control him. Rightly so. He's never come to our home, no matter how many times I've invited him when he's in town. And I doubt he ever will. *But* he is so good to me in every other way. And how wonderful that he's been with me here for a while. He ran the place by himself when I was in the hospital. Jax spoils me."

And how do you repay his kindness? By taking his money every month when you have millions stashed away.

"He's a very special man," Brooke said.

"Yes." Her penetrating gaze was knowing. "I haven't missed how you look at him."

"I…" An involuntary blush heated her cheeks. "He's pretty easy on the eyes."

"He is that. And you're plain gorgeous, Brooke. I see how he looks at you, too. I'm not getting any younger. Hurry up and give me some grandbabies. They're bound to be beautiful."

Wouldn't that be lovely? Brooke widened her eyes as if stunned by Sofia's request.

Sofia cackled at Brooke's feigned discomfort.

"What's so funny, ladies?" Jax appeared at the counter.

"Just telling Brooke…"

She narrowed her eyes at Sofia and gave her a subtle wag of her head.

"Girl talk," Sofia said. "Why don't you two have some breakfast? I think we're about done for the day."

"Sounds good to me. Are you hungry, Brooke?"

"Yep. Pops' Special hungry." She hopped off of the stool.

"Go pick out a booth and I'll order the food," he

said.

As usual, Brooke enjoyed the meal and Jax's company too much. She ended her work day bound for her empty apartment with an over-full stomach and threatened heart break. So far it appeared that Sofia might face jail time and, if so, Brooke's future with Jax was pure fantasy.

Mike had left her a note thanking her for the possible intel. He wrote that he'd analyze the data on the flash drive after work. She checked her watch, and her frustration mounted. She'd have to fill several hours before she could tell him about what she had learned from interviewing Sofia. Jax had promised to help Hunter paint a remodeled bathroom, so she couldn't spend time with him pretending that permanent separation didn't loom over them.

The weather was beautiful, though. So she changed into a bathing suit and cover up, slipped on flip flops and packed a tote bag with a couple beach towels filched off the sofa, sunscreen and a paperback. She'd laze on the beach for a while and then she'd use the coin op washing machines and dryers in the complex's laundry room to wash towels and sheets.

****

Mike's key rattled in the lock and her scowling partner walked through the door. "Smells better in here."

"Yeah," Brooke said. "I washed the dish towel and the towels covering the sofa cushions. Smells like fabric softener."

"Thanks." Mike tossed the rental car key onto the kitchen counter and then took his cell phone out of his pocket. "Want me to order Chinese for delivery?"

"Sure. Just the crab Rangoon for me. I'm still full. I

ate at the café after my shift."

Mike placed the online delivery order and then disappeared down the hall. He came back into the front room toting his laptop and the flash drive. Brooke sat down on the sofa and played puzzle games on her cell phone while he worked at the kitchen counter.

The food order had yet to arrive when he closed his computer.

She raised her head and looked in his direction. "Well?"

"Nothing new here."

"What does that mean? Is he in the clear?"

"Do you know if this is his only computer?"

"No. I'd guess yes. But I didn't get the chance to search the rest of his condo. Nothing suspicious on there?"

"Nothing useful."

"I have something that's very useful after interviewing Sofia today."

Brooke relayed her conversation with Sofia in detail.

"I agree. That's *very* useful. Good work. Submit a report."

"Okay. How are you doing at Mercury?"

He frowned. "I haven't gotten anywhere near Baxter's office or the central computer room yet. My ID badge is useless. I'm working on hacking in from here. I'll get there in time."

Brooke knew that he would succeed. But how much time would it take? Every day she fell deeper in love with Jax and a clean break with him seemed more and more impossible.

"You know…" Mike tilted his head to the side, and

she could almost see his brain work behind his gray eyes. "I would *really* like to get into Baxter's mansion and check out any personal computers. Could you wangle an invitation for us from Sofia? I'm way too low on the totem pole at work to rate a personal invitation from the CEO."

Only if Jax is included and he will never go along with it. How much to reveal to Mike about Sofia's matchmaking without admitting that she would love to be "matched"? Better to leave all that out of the conversation.

"She's already invited us to dinner, but Jax went ballistic and refused to accept. He hasn't fully explained it to me yet, but he can't stand Thurston Baxter. Sofia confirmed that Jax has never set foot in the house that she lives in with his stepfather. We could have a TacOps team go in while the house is empty. Dad alluded to being willing to employ a team at our discretion. Sofia is out of her house from dawn until, I'd guess late afternoon. She has never left before me so far. The café's posted hours are from six in the morning until three thirty in the afternoon. She may or may not leave before three thirty. According to Jax, keeping open for lunch is a bust. Baxter leaves at the crack of dawn, too. So the team should gain access maybe at eight a.m. or so. That would give them three hours minimum to work."

"All right. I'll make the request to the director and see how fast they can assemble the team."

"So is Jax in the clear now?"

"Maybe. I'd like to take a closer look at him before I rule him out. Invite him to dinner."

"Here? Look at this place. Where would we sit?"

"I know it's a dump. But invite him anyway. Ask

him what kind of takeout he likes. There's nothing here to use to make a hot meal."

"We could always serve him toaster pastries."

Her sarcasm tickled Mike and he sputtered a laugh. "I don't think the toaster works."

Chapter 10

The crowded breakfast rush at Pops' Café flew by in a blur. Brooke didn't have a chance to talk to Jax until she was about to punch out. She stuck her head in the office where Jax was bent over paperwork on the desk and tapped her knuckles on the door frame. "Sorry to bother you."

Jax raised his head. A high watt smile lit his eyes. "You're never a bother."

"I wonder if you would like to have dinner with Mike and me tonight at our place."

Her invitation hung in the air at his hesitation.

"It's okay if you're busy. Maybe another time," she blurted out and turned away from the door.

"Brooke, wait."

She halted and faced him again.

"I'd love to come," he said. "I'm supposed to meet Hunter tonight at Peggy's Place to listen to the live band they have once a month. But I would much rather spend time with you. I'll work it out with Hunter."

"Are you sure?"

Jax nodded.

"Great. Does six-thirty work for you? Mike gets home late some nights."

"Sounds good. And if we feel like it, we can all go to Peggy's after dinner."

"Then it's a date. See you this evening."

Brooke seesawed between looking forward to the evening and regretting having extended Mike's required invitation to get a closer look at Jax. Would he read how she felt about Jax and how emotionally involved she had become? If he did, what did that mean for her career? For her uncertain future with the subject of their investigation? If the investigation proved that Jax was innocent as she believed he was, would that make a difference to her partner? To her superiors? To her father?

Would her astute partner see that she was falling in love with Jax?

She had no alternative but to carry through and hope for the impossible happy outcome. Brooke bought cheese, crackers and fruit for "appetizers" on her way home. Mike had volunteered to pick up wine and beer after work with a stop at a celebrated burger restaurant near Mercury Labs for takeout. The meal they'd provide for Jax was miles away from home cooked.

But who doesn't love burgers and fries?

Brooke strolled along Beach Boulevard on her way to the apartment, window shopping and basking in the balmy weather. A long white skirt, dotted with daisy appliques which hung in the window of a boutique caught her eye and she couldn't resist trying it on. Fifteen minutes later she breezed out of the store after buying the skirt, a new sweater and an adorable pair of shoes.

She enjoyed the normalcy of walking in the sunshine after some retail therapy. Maybe she could put the reality of her undercover relationship to Jax aside for just that night. Maybe she could enjoy some comfort food, go out dancing and pretend that she was on a date with a special man.

Brooke showered, carefully applied makeup, styled her hair in loose curls and dressed in her new outfit. She loved the fit and the way the skirt's soft material swished against her legs when she walked. After she clasped her heirloom daisy bracelet on her wrist, she took a quick mirror picture and added the photo, captioned My Impulse Buy, to a text to Kay.

—I am so stealing that outfit the next time we're together. You look amazing. —

She smiled at Kay's reply and went into the kitchen to set out her appetizer purchases, paper plates and napkins on the small counter. Brooke frowned at the mismatched bar stools and overall dilapidation of the place, an affront to her normally well-honed hostess instincts.

A couple of knocks on the door sounded, triggering butterflies to flutter inside her. She opened the door.

Jax stood outside clad in black, perfectly fitted jeans and a muscle-hugging powder blue, short sleeve tee. Her heart leaped at the loving expression in his eyes. He held out a huge bouquet of pale pink roses and beamed at her.

"Wow you look beautiful." He kissed her lips softly.

And you look sexy as hell.

"Thank you." She accepted the flowers and buried her nose in the delicate petals. "They smell like heaven. Let me put these in water."

Jax followed her into the kitchen and watched as she dug through all the cabinets until she found a chipped glass pitcher that she could make work. "This place really makes me miss my kitchen at home."

He pulled up a bar stool, shifting to strike a balance on its rickety footing and watched her arrange the flowers. Jax only gazed at her rather than at his dubious surroundings. *Smart guy.*

The door banged open, and Mike strode into the apartment, encumbered by takeout bags. Jax rose to meet him and took the bags out of Mike's hands.

"Hi Jax. Thanks. I'll be right back. I have beer and wine in the car."

Brooke emptied the bags and arranged the food on mismatched plates and in bowls that came along with their "furnished" rental.

Mike reentered the room with the beverages.

"This is a lot of food," Jax said to Mike. He crunched up a bag and tossed it in the trashcan.

Mike handed Jax a beer and took one for himself. He tossed a Diet Coke at Brooke which she caught one-handed. Jax arched his eyebrows at her. She grinned back, popped the top and took a swig. The trio settled at the counter.

"Hey Brooke. Remember the time Kay and I invited you to the condo for the first time?" Mike said.

"No I don't. Just eat." She popped a fry in her mouth.

He ignored her. "We decided we would order pizza, Jax. When the delivery guy came Brooke got into a heated argument with him claiming that it was the wrong order."

"You ordered one pizza, Mike. One. Jax if you had three people for dinner would you only order only one pizza? I mean, who does that?" She took a huge bite of her cheeseburger.

"Well. I would have to order at least two in case someone doesn't like mushrooms."

She grinned and nodded her head—case closed.

"Our dad always said that Brooke ate like a grizzly

bear just waking up from hibernation."

Jax barked a laugh.

Actually Mike had delivered that line when he had witnessed Brooke eating a plate of tacos in less than five minutes.

"You're lucky you don't have a brother, Jax." She snagged an onion ring off Mike's plate.

"This was good. And I'm full. Thank you." Jax rubbed his stomach.

Brooke grabbed the last onion ring, shoved off the stool and started stacking empty plates. She touched Jax's shoulder gently as he made to rise from his seat. "Stay where you are. I've got this. You guys relax."

Brooke cleared the way for Mike to question Jax about his mother and stepfather.

"How do you like the new job?" Jax said.

"Let's just say it's not what I expected." Mike took a swig of his beer. "Brooke told me your dad works at Mercury. Maybe I've met him."

"Not my dad, my mother's husband." Jax's tone was clipped. Brooke knew that Mike had hit a nerve.

"Oh sorry, I must have misunderstood. Anyway, I thought I would have more work to do. I was hired to straighten out some problems with AI development but my boss acts like I'm some kind of admin. I have a lot to contribute but he won't even let me in his office. He solely comes to my work station. It's crazy. I know they vetted me before they hired me, so trust should be a given. I've never worked for someone like Baxter."

"Baxter? You work for Thurston Baxter?"

"I was hired to work *with* Thurston Baxter, but I guess he didn't get the memo."

"Well good luck with that. He's my mother's

husband and he's a tough man to get along with. I don't know what my mother ever saw in him. I know she was lonely when I went to college. She must have been unbearably lonely to marry the likes of that asshole. He never treated her well even when she worked for him."

"Your mother worked for him?"

"Not for very long. He proposed and once they got married he turned into a caveman. No wife of his was going to work. It really pissed him off when my grandfather got sick, and my mom went back to work to take care of Pops' Café."

"Did your stepfather ever discuss work with you?"

Jax snorted. "I've never really engaged in conversation with the guy about anything. I feel sorry for you, Mike. I would never want to work for him. I can't stand him."

"Thanks for the honest insight, Jax. Pretty depressing. If things don't change soon, I might be looking for another job."

Mike's phone rang. Brooke picked it up off the counter and handed it to him.

He glanced at the screen and swiped to answer. "Hi love. Hold on a sec. I'm going to take this in my room, if you don't mind. You guys have fun tonight."

"We can wait for you if you want to come." Brooke hoped he'd decline. If he did, it meant that he didn't need to look into Jax further. And that Brooke could be alone with Jax without Mike's scrutiny.

"Thanks, but I'm beat. I'm looking forward to talking with my lady, taking a nice hot shower and then crashing in bed." He rose from the stool. "Great to see you, Jax. You're welcome any time."

"Alone at last." Jax stood behind Brooke at the sink

and nuzzled her neck.

She dried her hands on a towel and turned into his arms.

"Thank you for dinner." He kissed any response away.

Jax ended the sweet kiss.

"I'm glad you came even though this sorry place isn't up to my usual hosting standards. At all. Thank you for ignoring all that." She stood on tip toes and kissed him again.

"I enjoyed this. Especially the kisses." He brushed his lips on her crown. "I told Hunter we would try to be there before the band started. We'll make it if we leave now. I think you'll like the country music band. Hunter and I went to high school with some of the guys."

"Sounds great, let me grab my phone and we can go."

****

The band was tuning up as Brooke and Jax strolled hand in hand over to Hunter's large table right next to the dance floor.

"Great seats." Brooke gave Hunter a hug.

"It pays to know the owner," he said.

Brooke circled the table to hug Lyndsey, Nick and Mavis.

"Jax didn't tell me you would be here, Mavis. It's so good to see you again." Brooke sat down next to her.

"I love your skirt. Where did you find it?" Mavis said.

"Thanks. I saw it in the window of a little boutique near my apartment and had to have it."

"Oh look Mavis. It matches Brooke's bracelet," Lyndsey said.

Brooke held out her arm displaying the treasure on her wrist. "It was my mom's bracelet. That's why I just had to have the skirt."

There were pitchers of beer and one pitcher of Diet Coke on the table. Jax poured them each a glass of Diet Coke. The band opened with Garth Brooks' "Friends In Low Places."

The crowd erupted singing along, Hunter's table included. Brooke joined right in delighting in the happy camaraderie. Every successive song spurred another sing along.

"Wow you guys know every word," Brooke said.

"This isn't our first rodeo," Jax teased. "Hunter and I have come to live band nights since we were in high school."

"C'mon Hunt, you've sat on your butt long enough. It's time to get your table out on the dance floor," the lead singer joked.

The band started playing the Blanco Brown song "The Git Up" and a cheer went up from the crowd.

Jax held out his hand. "Want to dance?"

"I sure do."

He taught Brooke the steps and she quickly picked up on the dance. The band played a collection of line dance tunes, and they all kicked, stomped and slid along with the music. Mavis and Nick left the dance floor and walked back to the table followed by Hunter and Lyndsey, leaving Brooke and Jax alone. They started to head back to the table when the band played the Josh Turner song "Your Man."

"Oh, this is my favorite song," Brooke said.

Jax put his hands around her waist and pulled her close. She encircled her arms around his shoulders and swayed in his arms. He kissed her neck softly and sang the song in her ear.

His voice was low and gravelly, and it vibrated through her body.

Brooke would look back on that moment as the exact time that she fell head over heels in love with Jax. She raised her head off his chest. As if in slow motion, he lowered his head and kissed her. His lips played with hers igniting deep desire. Locked in the embrace, they stopped moving to the music and stood in the middle of the dance floor oblivious to anyone around them. The only thing that mattered was Jax's kisses. She wanted to stop time and stay in his arms forever.

Whistling and clapping snapped her back to reality. They were the only people left on the dance floor and the band had taken a break.

Brooke put her hand on her flaming cheek. "I'm so embarrassed."

Jax's laughter was contagious, and she laughed, too. He clasped her hand, bowed to the crowd, tugged her off the dance floor, tossed a good night out to Hunter et al and kept leading her right out the door.

She was breathless when they reached the car. He leaned over the center console in the front seat. "One more kiss."

He screeched out of the parking lot leaving her with her head spinning happily.

"Thank you for tonight. I can't remember the last time I had this much fun." Jax squeezed her hand.

"Thank *you*. For coming to dinner and dancing with me. I've never had someone sing to me. That was special."

"My pleasure."

They listened to a country station to keep the vibe going on the drive to her apartment. Brooke refused to think about anything other than the wonderful time that she had.

Wonderful continued when he parked in front of her building and kissed her again, deepening the kiss when she responded by pressing toward him and tangling her fingers in his soft hair.

He withdrew his lips and trailed his fingers down the sides of her face.

"I can't get enough of you, Brooke. If you're not busy Friday night, come to dinner at my place."

Brooke knew that dinner meant much more, and that she should probably avoid being alone with Jax with his bedroom nearby. But she was in love with him. When the case was over she'd find a way for them to be together.

"I would love that. Good night, Jax." She opened her door and got out of the car.

On her doorstep, Brooke turned and waved goodbye to him, already counting the minutes until Friday night.

Chapter 11

Mike lumbered in to the apartment without a word of acknowledgment to Brooke who sat on the sofa facing him. He tossed his keys on the countertop, opened the fridge, took out a beer, popped the top, and drank probably half the can before he gazed in her direction.

"Well hello to you, too, partner." Her sarcasm had him scowling.

"Hey, Brooke." His gentle tone belied the miffed expression on his face.

"Rough day?" she said.

"No. But I'm pretty tired." He took a sip of beer. "It's been a really good day, actually. We've got 'em, Brooke."

Her head spun. The Op was over? Who exactly was "them"? *Please not Jax.*

She rose from the couch. "Have they been arrested?"

"Not yet. But don't go to work tomorrow morning. It will probably go down then. Washington is coordinating the arrest with the L.A. office."

"This is amazing. Great work, Mike." She itched to know Jax's fate. If there was any chance that she could protect him, she would.

But no matter how she felt about him, she'd never look the other way if Mike had tied him to criminal traitorous activity with his family.

Brooke drifted into the kitchen and got herself a Diet

Coke which she had no real desire to drink. She sat down next to Mike.

"They'll arrest the whole family?" Her voice cracked a bit, but Mike didn't seem to notice.

"No. Sofia and Thurston Baxter. Jax has been cleared."

Jax is cleared. Jax is cleared. Jax is cleared! The beautiful mantra repeated in her head.

"I'm supposed to go to dinner with Jax tonight. Should I?"

He narrowed his eyes. "You didn't mention that."

"I didn't? I thought I had updated you the other day. Anyway… are we out of here? Should I cancel?"

Mike tilted his head and pursed his lips, a pensive expression on his face. "No. Business as usual. All the pieces aren't in place yet. We don't want to tip his mother and stepfather off and give them time to rabbit on us."

"I'm pretty sure he'd arrest his stepfather himself. But you're right about Sofia. He'd protect her at all costs."

Brooke checked her watch. "Think I'll take a quick shower. Is there anything you need me to do now to help you?"

"Nope." He crushed the beer can with his fist. "When you come back tonight, pack up. Tentatively we fly home tomorrow morning early."

"Gotcha." She left the room bound for the hall bathroom.

Inside the tiny room, she put down the commode seat and sat on it, head in hands, tears welling. They'd leave tomorrow. She couldn't forewarn Jax. The arrests had to go down as planned. Brooke couldn't risk saying goodbye to him and trying to make some sort of plan to see each other again. How could she leave him when he had come to mean the world to her?

Maybe things could somehow work out in time. Doubtful. But Brooke had to cling to that slim hope.

She raised her head and swiped away tears vowing to enjoy every last second she might have with him. For that night, she wasn't undercover Special Agent Brooke Pellington. Brooke James would remain a breakfast waitress for the café owner's son for one more night. A woman in love with a special man.

Brooke lingered under the shower spray letting the pounding water blank her mind, relieved that at least she didn't have to snoop around Jax's condo behind his back anymore. She'd take that gain at face value and not overthink the rest.

She wanted to look pretty for him—alluring. Because if dinner at his place led to his bedroom, she wanted to surrender to her powerful attraction to him. Brooke wanted not only an intimate night with Jax but rather scores of nights and days and years. *Maybe.*

Just in case, Brooke unmade her bed before she left her room anticipating the possibility that she might not make it home from Jax's house before Mike came looking for her in the early morning. She could always claim she took a predawn jog after a sleepless night.

****

When Jax answered her doorbell ring looking gorgeous and irresistible, tears threatened again. Brooke used all her professional discipline to tamp them down and instead smiled radiantly at him.

"Wow," he said.

"Wow yourself." She held out a bottle of wine that

the shop owner had insisted was "delectable on the pallet." Brooke needed a *big* glass, delectable or not.

Jax ushered her inside and offered her a bar stool seat so they could talk while he finished preparing dinner. He uncorked the wine and poured two glasses.

"Smells like heaven in here. What are you cooking?" She swirled a baby carrot in hummus and crunched on it.

"One of my specialties: beef Wellington with twice baked potato and green beans almondine. I hope you like it."

"Whoa. And that's just one specialty? You really are a man of many talents."

I wish I could welcome him to my place and wow him with my cooking. Longing to open her door to him some evening and share her home, her talents, her everything with Jax swamped her. *Maybe someday.*

He grinned at her, snapping her out of her melancholy, took his cell phone in hand and tapped on the screen a couple times. The sound of Josh Turner's voice filled the room…*Your man.*

"Aw…" The lovely memory of him singing what she'd come to think of as their song to her a few days ago remained fresh and romantic in her mind. She'd never forget it. "I had such a nice time at Peggy's Place with you."

Jax gave her a slow, sexy smile. "Same."

He picked up a potholder in each hand and took the roast out of the oven. The crust that wrapped around the beef tenderloin was decorated with pastry cutouts of leaves. The dish looked photo ready for a food magazine.

"My mouth is watering, Jax. No bag of burgers at your house. Gosh, I'm mortified that's all we served you the other night."

"Don't be. I love a good burger. And that was a good burger." He gave her a slow smile, his eyes soft, beckoning her. "Want to dance with me while this cools enough to carve?"

Brooke didn't hesitate. She popped up from the stool and met him as he rounded the kitchen bar into the great room. Jax took her in his arms and held her close tucking her head under his chin.

Floating in a sensual haze, Brooke immersed in the sheer intoxication of having Jax's strong arms around her. The pleasure of the moment was almost enough to push aside dwelling on what likely would happen the next morning to blow Jax's life apart and bury dreams of a future with him. She wanted to pretend tomorrow wouldn't come. And she could after she had executed just one more undercover act that evening.

The song ended and they stood in place, their gazes locked as if the potent desire coursing between them melded them to each other.

"Your beautiful meal is getting cold." Brooke didn't move to break the embrace.

"I hope not." Jax didn't move, either.

She stood on tiptoe and brushed a kiss on his lips. "I'm starving."

"Can't have that."

He let her loose and went back to the kitchen. Brooke resumed sitting on the bar stool watching him. When Jax turned his back on her to work at the stove, she nabbed his phone off the counter, switched it off and laid it back down in the same place.

Special Agent Brooke Pellington's job was officially done.

Brooke closed her eyes trying to compartmentalize the surge of guilt brought by her dishonesty with Jax. She exalted in falling in love with him even though she knew that she never should have as a professional. But having found what she believed was forever love, Brooke deeply regretted the damage that tomorrow's arrests would do to their hearts. A shudder passed through her knowing that she'd get on a plane with Mike the next morning and disappear without explanation or apology to Jax.

Tomorrow is tomorrow. I won't think about this until then.

Jax faced her. "Dinner is served."

"Oh boy." Brooke rose to her feet holding out her arms. "Here. Let me help you carry things."

He lit a candle on the table, pulled out a chair for her and placed a cloth napkin on her lap with a flourish. Seated across from her, he filled her plate and then one for himself. Jax's eyes roved the table's surface and then he half rose from his seat.

"Where are you going?"

Her question halted his motion. "I left my phone on the counter. I want to put some more music on."

She reached across the table and touched his arm. "I can use my phone to connect to your speaker."

Jax sat back down. "Great. Choose whatever you'd like to listen to."

Brooke queued up a romantic instrumental playlist and then set her phone down on the table. The delicious candlelit dinner while love songs played in the background was the prelude to acting on the powerful attraction between them. She wasn't her job then. Brooke was a woman deeply in love. She wanted Jax—that much about Brooke James was one hundred percent honest.

The melody to "Lady in Red" played through the room's speakers. He pointed to her. "And what do you know? You're wearing red. Want to dance again?"

"Yes."

Brooke didn't hold back, enfolded in his arms. When he molded her body close to his, she pressed closer into the embrace melding their bodies together. Consuming heat built between them and their lips fused. He slipped his hands under her shirt skimming his fingers over her back sending delicious chills through her.

"Off," she muttered against his lips.

Cool air bathed her exposed skin as he pulled the top off over her head. He yanked off his POLO shirt and locked her in his arms again tenderly running his hand up and down her back and arms. In the next breathless moment her feet left the ground as Jax lifted her into his arms and carried her to his bedroom.

Candlelight flickered in that room, too. Jax had set the stage for seduction, obviously wanting her as much as she wanted him. Nothing else mattered to Brooke but the mind shattering ecstasy of making love with Jax.

They fell asleep in each other's arms. She awakened to soft kisses and responded to his advance again not caring about the time or the Op or the sure knowledge that the more she gave herself to him and greedily accepted his giving himself to her, the higher looming devastation.

Disoriented, she awoke again in a pitch-dark room. Jax lay sleeping next to her with his chest exposed, one muscled arm extended over his head on the pillow. She resisted running her hand over the smooth planes of his torso one last time.

She inched out of his bed in slow increments and fished her articles of clothing off the floor. She stood naked with her clothes draped over her arm watching him sleeping. Brooke longed to kiss him awake and lose herself with him one more time. At least she could kiss him goodbye. But no. She could actually feel her heart fracture in her chest.

Aching, she leaned closer to him. "I love you. I'm sorry," she mouthed.

Brooke tiptoed out of his bedroom. She dressed in the great room and gathered her things. Her phone screen illuminated the digital time when she picked it up off of the dinner table—1:00 a.m. A text message notification from Mike displayed.

She swiped up on her phone, unlocked it with face I.D. and tapped on the text message icon.

—*Got all my work done, sis. See you in the morning*—

Done. That concluded her work. As she soundlessly let herself out the door of Jax's condo she prayed that somehow what was done wouldn't conclude them.

Chapter 12

Jax outstretched his right arm, reaching for Brooke. Her side of the bed was empty. Maybe he remembered her leaving his bedroom at some point in the middle of the night. He brought her pillow to his nose and inhaled the light scent of honeysuckle and coconut stifling a laugh at his instant erection. Damn, he felt like a teenage boy hot and bothered by a girl's perfume for the first time. It was three a.m. according to the clock on his bedside table. He had another hour left before he had to get up for work, so he pulled the sheets up and went back to sleep.

The sound of his bedroom door slamming against the wall roused Jax. Hunter stood in the doorway with his hands on his hips like a parent about to yell at his kid.

"What the hell are you doing here Hunter?"

Jax's question was met with a question. "Why haven't you answered your phone? It's ten o'clock. When I didn't find you at Pops' I thought you were dead or something."

"Ten o'clock? Damn. I never oversleep." He tossed off the bedcovers, strode into the bathroom and stepped into the shower without even taking the time to let the water heat up. The cold stream over his body jolted him fully awake.

When he rushed into the kitchen, Hunter was still there in his condo. He apparently had made coffee, filled a large mug and had set it on Jax's counter. Hunter was busy scraping and rinsing plates and loading them into the dishwasher.

KP was the last thing on Jax's mind the night before. "You don't have to do that. I'll take care of it after work. I have to get to the restaurant. Have you seen my phone?"

"Yeah. Over there." Hunter pointed to the far end of the counter.

Jax picked up the phone. "I don't remember turning my phone off, but I must have. No wonder I didn't hear my alarm this morning." He powered up the device.

"Or any of my texts or phone calls either. Gee. I have so many missed calls and messages. What the hell is going on?"

"Your mother was arrested."

"What? Why?" Jax's jaw dropped.

"Maybe you better sit down." Hunter slid the mug of coffee over to Jax.

Jax sat down on the edge of a counter stool. "When did this happen?"

"Around dawn, I think. She's okay, Jax. Really shook up, though."

"I can't believe I slept through all of this. Where are they holding her?"

"She's home now. I don't know the whole story, but my dad just called. He said the FBI raided Baxter's and your mom's house early this morning and arrested them both. Baxter lawyered up immediately, but he's accused of espionage and selling trade secrets to the Chinese. An undercover FBI agent posing as a Chinese buyer worked the investigation along with undercover agents at Mercury Labs."

"Wow. I always knew that guy was poison. My poor

mom."

"Yeah, well there's more, Jax. He apparently passed the money through an account in your mom's name."

"That son of a bitch. I want to kill him. What's going to happen to Mom?"

"She's been released to her lawyer's custody because Baxter exonerated her. At least he did the honorable thing where she's concerned. And the FBI gathered proof that he forged her signature in setting up the account. She called you when they let her go, but when you didn't answer, she called my parents."

Guilt swamped Jax. While his mom went through horrible trauma, he was dreaming about making love to Brooke. "I should have been there for her."

"My dad called Chuck, his lawyer. He was with your mother when they questioned her. My mom drove her home when she was released. I think she's still with her at her house now."

"My head is spinning. I don't know what to say. Thank you, Hunter. I owe you and your parents big time."

"Come on, no thanks needed. We're family. You know I'd do anything for you, except clean that roasting pan. That's where I draw the line." He chuckled and patted Jax on the back. "I have to go to work. If you or your mom need anything just call."

"Thanks again." As soon as the door closed behind Hunter, Jax dialed his mother's cell phone. His call went right to voicemail. She didn't respond to a text message he sent to her phone so he sent a text to Hunter's mom.

She responded immediately.

—Hi honey, I finally got your mom to lie down, and she just dozed off. I turned her phone off. I'll stay here

with her and let you know when she wakes up.—

His fingers flew over his phone's keypad.

—I can't thank you enough. I'm sorry you couldn't reach me. I'll be at Pops' if you need me.—

Jax smiled at the thumbs up and heart emojis she sent in response. He punched in the number for Pops'.

His call was answered on the fourth ring. "Good morning, Pops' Café. How may I help you?" came a deep voice.

"Good morning. This is Jax. Who's this?"

"It's Ed Kelly. Jax my boy, everyone has been trying to get in touch with you. Are you okay?"

"I'm fine, Mr. Kelly. My phone was off. I missed all the calls and my morning alarm. How come you answered my call there?"

"Things were crazy when the boys and I showed up this morning. Sergio was frazzled so we offered to help. Reminded me of the time your grandpa pulled his back helping to unload a truck; we pitched in and helped then, too."

"Well, thank you. I'm on my way. Can you put Brooke on the phone for a minute please?"

"Brooke isn't here. She didn't show up this morning, either. I think Sergio tried to call her, but I'm not sure. You'll have to ask him when you get here. Got to run. Dan is trying to snake my tip off a table."

Jax barked a laugh as the call disconnected. He grabbed his wallet and keys and headed out the door. As soon as he got in the car he dialed Brooke's number. It went straight to a default voicemail. "Hey Brooke. It's Jax, I guess your alarm didn't wake you, either. I'm on my way to Pops'. I think we have everything handled so you can take the day off if you want. I have a few fires I have to put out today, but I'll call you later." He paused.

"I just wanted to say that last night was…*amazing, fantastic, a dream come true, mind blowing* …well I just wanted to tell you, it was perfect."

****

The sound of shattering glass brought Brooke from a deep sleep to upright at the side of her bed ready to ward off attack in a split second. She ran out of her room into the living room and found Mike standing at the sink swearing like a sailor.

"What happened? Are you okay?" Her heart pounded in her chest.

"Sorry to wake you. I'm fine. I broke the coffee pot. It hit the faucet as I tried to fill it with water." He used paper towels to scoop up the glass and dump it into the garbage. "You got in late last night. I fell asleep on the couch waiting for you."

"I didn't want to wake you. Figured you needed the sleep. How did the arrest go?" She leaned against the counter and covered a yawn with her hand.

"Everything went according to plan. We can talk about it over breakfast. I need coffee. I'll run and get us something. Why don't you shower while I'm gone? We have to pack and get out of here this morning." He grabbed the car keys. "What do you want to eat?"

"An egg and sausage croissant with cheese would be great." Her stomach growled.

Mike grinned at her. "I'll make it two sandwiches, an order of hash browns and a quart of coffee. I'll be right back."

"You know I love you, right?" She smiled as he walked out the door and she headed towards the shower.

Brooke let the hot water beat down on her back as

she washed and conditioned her hair. Her phone vibrated on her dresser as she pulled on a pair of leggings. She donned a well-worn Indiana University sweatshirt and then grabbed the phone off the dresser. Her heart fluttered as she listened to Jax's voicemail. Last night certainly was a night that dreams were made of. Jax summed it up; last night was perfect. She hoped he'd cling to that, as she would, until she had a chance to explain everything to him.

Brooke towel dried her hair and twisted it up into a bun on the top of her head. She padded into the kitchen, sat at the counter and looked at Mike's open laptop scanning the report from the U.S. Marshal's office which had assisted in the arrests early that morning. Thank God Jax's mother was released into her lawyer's custody without having to post bail. Brooke didn't know how long it would take, but she was positive that Sofia wouldn't stand trial. Brooke hoped that once Sofia was fully cleared, Jax would understand Brooke's part in the investigation when everything came out at the Grand Jury hearing. More importantly, she prayed that he would forgive her for ghosting him. Because after breakfast that was what she would do.

Brooke jumped up when she heard Mike's key in the door, closed Mike's laptop and set paper plates and napkins out on the counter.

She took a giant bite of the sandwich that Mike placed on her plate. "This is so delicious," she mumbled with her mouth full. "Thanks."

"You're welcome."

He let out a laugh watching her finish a sandwich before he had a chance to take the first bite of his food. "You know, I'm really going to miss being your roommate. I kind of liked having you as my sister."

"Once you marry Kay, who is my sister by different parents, I promise you'll get sick of me. Who knows? We might wind up on another assignment together." Brooke took smaller bites of her second sandwich.

"How did your dinner go with Jax last night? You seem awful hungry."

"He made a great dinner."

"Didn't you eat it?"

She popped a large piece of hash brown into her mouth. "We got interrupted."

"Interrupted, how?"

"A song came on that we danced to the other night, and he asked me to dance."

"And what? You didn't eat after the dance? Oh wait, never mind. I don't think I want to know what you did after the dance."

"No, you don't want to know."

"Your father called last night. He said he tried your phone, and you didn't answer. He wasn't pleased. The call was to tell us we have a few days off before we have to report for our next assignment."

"Kay must be thrilled."

"She had to work the late shift in the NICU last night, so I haven't told her yet. I'm going to surprise her." He stood and started to collect the plates and napkins. "What will you do with the free time?"

What would she do or what would she *like* to do? She would like to stay in California for a few days to be with Jax. But she couldn't jeopardize their case until Baxter was indicted. "I don't know yet. Maybe go hang out at the house on the Bay."

"You could come with me if you want." He wiped

down the counter.

"Thank you, but no. You never have enough time alone with Kay. I'm not going to horn in on your few days together."

"Well if you change your mind, it's an option. Now let's get out of this dump."

They parted and went into their rooms to pack up their things.

Brooke called her father's office after they had cleaned out the apartment and they were in the car on their way to the airport. She was on hold for five minutes before he finally picked up the call.

"Good morning sir. Mike told me you called last night."

"I did and I fully expected you to answer. Unacceptable."

"I understand, sir but I was working, and I turned my phone to silent."

"When I call, Special Agent, you will answer. Without exception."

Wasn't the call to tell me about a mini vacation? What's the big deal?

She swallowed an argumentative retort. "It won't happen again, sir. Yes sir, he did tell me about the days off. Thank you, sir. Yes, I will be at the meeting."

Brooke sighed and dumped her phone in her lap.

"Well that went great." Mike laughed breaking the dead silence in the car.

"Yeah well…" She squeezed his hand resting on the console between them and closed her eyes for the rest of the drive, her heart shattering a little more with each passing mile away from Jax.

Chapter 13

Jax still couldn't reach Brooke after several attempts on his way to the restaurant. Her strange unavailability grew more ominous each time he had tried her number.

He disconnected yet another call to her cell phone leaving him even more disoriented than the time before. Since Hunter had relayed what had happened to his mother and her husband Jax had plunged into a surreal world. Even more perplexing, instead of routing his recent calls to Brooke's voicemail box a robotic voice informed him that her number was no longer in service.

Boiling inside with worry about the two most important women in his life, Jax parked behind Pops' Café and rushed inside the building.

Sergio worked the grill like a madman, but he gave Jax a lazy smile as if it were just another day at the restaurant. "Hey, man," he said. "Big night last night or something?"

"Or something." Jax tied an apron around his waist. "Thanks for holding things together."

"No problem, Jax. But Ed Kelly and the gents deserve the credit. Where's Brooke?"

"Good question. I better go relieve the old boys."

He sauntered toward the swinging door ready to shove out into the dining room when his phone chirred. Reading the caller I.D. stopped him in his tracks—"Mom."

Jax swiped to answer the call. "Dear God, Ma. Are you okay? I can't believe any of this."

Sofia sobbed softly. "Oh, Jax. This is a nightmare. I'm so worried about Thurston."

"Um…I'm worried about *you*." He bit back a nasty retort about Baxter. Jax had no sympathy for the man after what he had brought down on his sweet mother. "This is a terrible shock and you're still recovering."

She sniffled, but thankfully she stopped crying. "I'll admit my heart was in my mouth through most of this. Especially when the FBI and the US Marshal got us out of bed and even handcuffed us. Oh my God, it was horrible, Jax."

He shuddered at the mental image. "I don't understand any of this. Did they give you a full explanation of why they arrested you and him?"

"Not really, although Chuck Roberts is going to get us details. They kept asking questions about a savings account. I kept telling them I don't even have a savings account—only checking. Since I married Thurston he takes care of all our banking and stuff."

Son of a bitch. "I understand from Hunter that he explained all that to the authorities and that's why they released you."

"Yes. My Thurston would never do anything to hurt me."

That's debatable. I want to strangle him. "I'm glad he did the right thing," Jax choked out. "Do you want me to come over there? I can close the restaurant early."

"No. Please stay and work the rush for me? The last thing I want is for the business to suffer any more than it already does. Peggy is still here with me if I need anything."

His mother seemed more composed, so Jax didn't press her, even though he itched to just hug her and love all this mess away. "Sure thing, Ma. Get some rest. Okay if I come over later?"

"Maybe for dinner?" No mistaking the delight in her voice. "And bring Brooke. I'll make my stuffed shells."

Thurston wasn't home and based on Hunter's explanation of what went down with the authorities that morning, he might never live in his *Architectural Digest* style mansion again. "Sure, Ma. That would be great. See you later."

"Oh boy. I'll get to work cooking. Thank you, Jax."

"Thank you? For what?"

"Everything you do for me. I really appreciate it, and I love you." She sniffled again bringing home how stressful and upsetting Baxter's betrayal was to her.

Jax wanted to wring the SOB's neck. "I love you, too, Ma. Don't work too hard."

He disconnected the call, pocketed his phone and almost crashed into Ed as both men made to go through the door between the kitchen and dining room from opposite directions at the same time.

"Whoa." Ed pulled up short. "Hey, Jax. Glad to see ya."

"Same here. Whatcha got there?" He eyed the scrap of paper in Ed's hand.

"Table 12's order." Ed handed Jax the note. "I write everything down like Pops did. I'm not good with that newfangled thingy."

Aka, iPad.

Jax chuckled. "I'll take it from here, Ed. Have you guys had time for breakfast?"

"Nope. And I'm starving."

"Go sit down and round up the gents. I'll bring your meals. Breakfast's on me—heck, for the rest of the month for covering for me."

"No need, my boy." Ed patted his pocket. "I made a pretty penny on tips this morning. So did the rest of us. You can sleep in anytime."

Ed grinned and then retreated back into the dining room. Jax read table 12's order to Sergio. He didn't need to give his cook Ed Kelly's and his friends' breakfast orders. They ate the same meal every single day for the past who knows how many years.

Jax juggled front of the house duties for the second seating, taking orders and delivering food for the rest of the rush. Things got so frenetic at one point that Sergio occasionally delivered food to tables himself before rushing back into the kitchen.

Still the time dragged despite his busyness. All Jax could think about was finding Brooke and making sure she was all right.

Jax pulled into the parking lot of Deluxe Apartment Homes, cut the engine and laughed out loud. After having spent some time in Brooke's and Mike's place there, he'd never pass the complex's signage again without bursting out laughing. His definition of deluxe had forever changed.

Despite his eagerness to see Brooke and find out what was wrong with her phone, he sat in the driver's seat, his forearms resting on the wheel and his brain buzzing. He couldn't shake the feeling that something was very wrong with Brooke despite the euphoric night they had spent together.

Was it just last night? It seemed like their perfect time together had happened a long time ago. He opened the car door, fervently hoping that he'd find her at home, apologetic about sleeping in and maybe setting up a new phone.

Jax slipped out of the car, slammed the door shut and hustled through the lot. He bounded up the steps leading to her door two at a time. His doorbell ring echoed from inside. After a couple minutes wait with no response, he rang the bell again. No answer. He pressed the button repeatedly setting off a cacophony of chimes that echoed a racket inside the apartment and then he stopped the futile exercise.

Before he gave up, he tested the door knob, surprised to find it unlocked. Maybe Brooke was around on the property somewhere doing laundry. Maybe her phone was broken, and she ran out to fix it or buy a new one. But if she was all right, why wouldn't she have shown up for work that morning? And why would she have left her front door unlocked unless she was inside, for some reason avoiding him at her front door.

One way to find out.

He stepped through the doorway calling out her name. She didn't answer.

Jax tromped down the narrow hallway and entered the first bedroom he came to—apparently Mike's from the slight scent of aftershave that lingered there. He did a one-eighty back out into the hallway. The second bedroom off the hall had to be Brooke's. Jax walked into the room.

Maybe he could detect the floral scent of Brooke's perfume. Maybe he was wishful thinking. Like in Mike's room, the bed was made; and the surfaces of the bureau and bedside table were empty. He marched over to the chest of drawers opening and shutting each one in rapid succession. Empty. Jax shoved open the closet sliding door and found it empty, too. He made a last-ditch attempt to prove that she still lived in the place searching the bedside table. The whole apartment was empty leaving Jax feeling powerless and deeply troubled.

He retraced his steps through the small unit, barreled out the door, traveled down the stairs and then followed the signs for "Model apartments" hoping to speak with someone who might help him.

Jax felt lucky for the first time that day when he found a live human being sitting behind a desk in the musty smelling management front office.

"Hello," Jax said. "I'm looking for my girlfriend, Brooke James, um in Unit C 2. I checked first and didn't find her home."

"Yep." The bespeckled, greasy haired man seated at the desk didn't bother to meet Jax's gaze. "Checked out early this morning." He pointed to his right. "Left their keys in that drop box. Good thing they were paid up on the rent, so I didn't have to hunt them down. People generally can't be trusted."

The information hit Jax like a jab to the solar plexus. He could barely squeak out, "Thanks. Sorry to bother you."

Back in his car, he propped his elbow on the wheel and kneaded his forehead with his hand. *Brooke, where are you?* The mantra repeated in his mind.

Keen to find answers, he fished his cellphone out of his pocket, googled Mercury Labs and called the general number.

"Mercury Labs, how may I direct your call?" came a singsong female voice.

"Um, good afternoon. This is, um, Thurston

Baxter's stepson," he choked out hoping his call might receive priority. "I need to speak with Mike James in IT."

She didn't immediately acknowledge his request nor transfer the call. He was about to say something when she responded, "Mr. James no longer works here."

"*What?* Since when?"

He heard papers rustling. "I believe he resigned at the end of the work day yesterday."

Jax tried, but failed, to wrap his mind around the information. "Can you please put me through to your human resources manager?"

"I'm sorry, sir, but she's not available."

What good would it do to press the woman further? "I understand. Thank you anyway."

"My pleasure sir. Is there anything else I can help you with?"

"Um…" *Tell me where I can find him and his sister? Explain to me what the hell is going on? Bring Brooke back to me?*

"No, thank you. Have a nice afternoon."

"You, too sir."

Jax didn't know what else to do, so he switched on the car's engine and drove to his condo. Maybe she left him a note or something and in his haste to get to the café he had overlooked it. Back home, he inspected every surface, threw off his bedcovers on the chance she had left a note on her pillow and checked his bathroom's and the powder room's counters. Brooke had disappeared without a trace.

His mouth went dry, so he grabbed a bottled water out of the fridge and stepped through his sliding glass door out onto his beachfront deck. Seated there, he unloaded his problems to Pops in his mind, desperately needing to receive his grandfather's guidance. Nothing came to him.

He gazed at the occasional jogger and beach walker. A possibility dawned. He raced inside, changed into workout gear and then hit the beach. He had met Brooke there by chance once. Maybe he'd find her again. And she'd explain that she had been evicted because Mike had lost his job. And she couldn't reach him because her phone service had been disconnected for non-payment. Jax should have cared enough to have asked about her finances. Maybe he could have helped her avoid all the upheaval.

One thing for sure. When he found her, he'd tell her that he'd give her a raise at the café. And she and Mike could move into his place. Or if it was too small, he'd ask Ma if maybe they could move in there until Mike found a new job. Ma would go for that. With Baxter away, she'd probably feel lonely.

His good intentions evaporated the longer he jogged. Brooke wasn't there on the beach. Brooke was gone.

Chapter 14

Brooke stowed her garment bag and bulging backpack in the overhead bin, slipped into her aisle seat, pulled the hood of her sweatshirt up over her head and slouched down, determined to sleep during the six-and-a-half-hour flight back to California to appear in front of the Grand Jury the next day. The team assigned to the Baxter case occupied the seats around her. Mike sat across the aisle from her with his laptop open going over their testimony. Brooke had her statements memorized. They would land after midnight and spend the night, what was left of it, in a hotel.

The flight took off. Brooke slid the shade down on the window and closed her eyes. She had spent the last few weeks in her house on the Chesapeake Bay commuting back and forth to the office in Washington D.C.. Every night when she closed her eyes she had dreamed about her pending reunion with Jax, itchy for word that the Grand Jury would convene in the Baxter case bringing them together again. Some nights in her dream world they had picked up right where they had left off and she had awakened happy. Other nights he had turned her away and she had awoken with tears streaming down her face.

Soon she'd see him in reality: a prospect that had her both wildly excited and filled with trepidation. Brooke had to believe that once she had explained why she couldn't contact him before then, he would forgive her for disappearing.

She had packed a few extra outfits hoping that she could spend a few days with him before she had to report back to work in D.C.. Happy musing about her future loving Jax openly as her true self lulled her into a deep, dreamless sleep. She didn't wake up until the wheels hit the tarmac on the West Coast.

****

Jax hunched with his elbows on his knees on the edge of the uncomfortable couch in his mother's formal living room. His hair stuck up all over his head from nervous finger combing. Edgy and antsy, he surged to his feet, paced down the hallway towards the den, stopped at the foot of the staircase and hollered up, "Everything okay Mom? Chuck should be here soon."

"I'll be down in a minute!"

Jax smiled. His mom's "minute" could take a half hour. Luckily they had plenty of time. But he wanted to get going, fast forward the day and put this whole mess behind them. He worried that the mounting stress was too much for Mom.

He drifted into the den and stood in front of the wall of wooden bookshelves. His mother's touch was everywhere in the room unlike the formal living room. Pops' big chair hulked in a corner. His mother had reupholstered the piece with the same dark blue material that had worn and faded over the years in Pops' house. Framed pictures perched among the books on the shelves. The photo of the Bama Boys from *Sports Illustrated* held a place of prominence. His mother had cut out and framed the article next to the picture of them hoisting the trophy.

Jax picked up a picture of him and his mom, who looked young and pretty, on the day he had made his First Communion. He could still feel the collar of that shirt choking him. Jax grinned at the family photo at Disneyland. Nana and Pops had treated him and Mom to tickets at the theme park. In the photo the four of them sported Mickey Mouse or Minnie Mouse ears laughing in front of the camera. He replaced the picture on the shelf and then picked up his all-time favorite. He and Pops stood in front of the fence at the town's Little League field. Jax held the ball that he had hit over that fence for his first homerun triumphantly overhead. He had convinced Pops to turn his hat around so they could look badass. Pops hadn't even yelled at Jax for swearing. He had tried valiantly to maintain a badass pose, but Pops wound up laughing in the picture. After he died, Mom had a copy of the photo made for Jax for Christmas and he treasured it.

He put the photo back on the shelf when he heard a car pull into the driveway.

"Mom, Chuck is here!" He hollered up the stairs on his way to the front door. No answer from the second floor.

Jax beat Baxter's manservant to the door. "I've got this." He dismissed the man and tugged the front door open.

"Hi Chuck. Come in. Mom said she would be down in a minute ten minutes ago. I'll run up and hurry her along. There's a fresh-brewed pot of coffee in the kitchen. Help yourself."

Jax took the stairs two at a time and hustled down the hallway to his mother's room. She sat on the side of her California king-sized bed, gripping her wedding day photo with her head bent, tears tracking down her cheeks.

He bit back his distaste for the man in that photo who had put his mother in a terrible situation. "Mom we have to go. Chuck is here."

"I know you don't like Thurston, honey. But I love him." She didn't break her gaze on the photo. "I can't believe he did the things they're accusing him of doing. He's not like that."

Her red-streaked eyes welling tears met his. The sight of her distress broke his heart. He wanted to tell her exactly what he thought of her husband, but he refused to add to her pain.

"I know you love him, Mom. Let's get you cleared and then we can see what we can do to help Baxter."

"You would help me prove his innocence?"

"Ma, I would do anything for you."

"Thank you, honey. You're such a good son." She stood up, swiped away tears with her hand, set the framed picture on the dresser and allowed Jax to usher her down the stairs.

The ride to Los Angeles dragged for Jax. He couldn't wait for the ordeal to end. Chuck evaded the Press assembled in front of the building, entering through a rear door of the towering Federal Courthouse. They went through security and made their way to the courtroom trailing Chuck. His mother's lawyer led them down a hallway lined with chairs and directed Jax and Mom to take seats opposite a pair of wooden doors guarded by a uniformed officer.

"Testimony is taken individually." Chuck instructed Sofia in soft tones. "I'm not allowed to go in with you; however, you can request to consult with me before answering a question if you're unsure of what to say. I'll be right here the whole time." He squeezed her hand. "It's going to be okay, Sofia. You didn't do anything wrong. Thurston has already taken full responsibility for his actions. This is just a formality."

One of the doors swung open and Sofia gave a start. A man emerged through the doorway, stomped down the hall, opened another door and called out, "Agent Pellington you're up."

Chuck consulted a slip of paper, running his finger down a list of names. "That should be the last testimony for the prosecution. Then it will be your turn, Sofia."

Jax's phone vibrated in his pocket signaling he had an email. He checked the phone expecting a response from work that morning since he had requested an extension of his leave the night before. His eyes were glued to his cell phone screen, and he barely registered movement into the hearing room in his peripheral vision. Jax caught a whiff of honeysuckle and looked up just as the door closed.

He read the email from his job. His boss had turned down his request for an extension of his leave and called for his resignation. The reply should have bothered Jax more than it did. His place right now was with his mother. He would find another job after the whole Baxter thing was behind her.

The door opened and a female officer called Sofia's name. Jax squeezed her hand. "Everything will be fine, Ma."

"She *is* going to be fine, Jax. Trust me." Chuck patted Jax's shoulder.

The lawyer's phone rang. "I have to grab this. Sofia, I'll be in this hallway if you need me." He walked away with the phone to his ear.

Jax rose to his feet and walked toward the double doors with Sofia. Her hand gripped his bicep, and he felt her shaking through the material of his blazer. The door opened in front of them revealing a smiling man and woman. Not just any woman—the woman who had blasted a hole in his heart.

Brooke. His eyes traveled down her body focusing on the name tag that she wore. It read, Special Agent Brooke Pellington.

He frowned, his heart racing. "What the hell is going on?"

"Brooke?" Sofia's face lit with her smile.

"Ma'am, please come with me," the officer directed Sofia.

Brooke and the man with her stepped into the hallway. The double doors closed sealing his mother inside the jury room and Jax outside in the hall face to face with the woman he loved.

The man with her assessed Jax's and Brooke's eye lock and said, "I'll wait for you in the car."

Jax watched him stride away. Large yellow letters: FBI on the back of his windbreaker had Jax putting the pieces together. He turned his gaze toward Brooke. She wore a badge on the waist band of her black slacks and a gun holster showed beneath the lapel of her tailored gray suit jacket.

Jax felt as if ice water coursed through his veins. "You're not Brooke James are you?"

She shook her head no and pointed to her name tag.

"Are you with the FBI?"

She nodded yes.

His heart splintered in his chest. "So it was all a lie.

You weren't interested in me at all. You used me to get to my mother."

Jax expected Brooke to argue against his assertions, but she just stood like a statue, mute and unsmiling.

"What kind of person does that? You wormed your way into our lives. We gave you a job. I introduced you to all my friends. We trusted you. I trusted you. You made me think... How do you sleep at night?" He inhaled a ragged breath and balled his fists at his sides. "No one goes after my mother. I will never forgive you for putting her through this."

He couldn't read the expression in her eyes as she just stood there, her lips pursed in a thin line.

"I have one more question for you. Do you always seduce your suspects?"

"Are you done?" Brooke whispered.

"Yes. I'm *done* with you."

Brooke turned her back on him and stepped away down the hall, her posture stiff.

****

Just keep walking. Don't let him know how much he hurt you.

Each word he had spewed at her had dealt a new blow. She felt the fool for expecting him to give her a chance to explain that she had worked to exonerate his mother in the face of damning evidence. And Jax, too.

She had to escape the building and Jax's disdain. Outside in the breezy sunshine, Brooke followed the sound of a honking horn and slipped into the back seat of the black SUV next to one of the IT guys. Mike sat in the driver's seat with another IT guy riding in the passenger seat. The mood was celebratory that they had done their parts in the successful Op.

Mike put the car in gear and pulled out into traffic. "We're going to grab lunch. Do you want to join us?"

"No thanks." The last thing Brooke could do was eat. "Could you drop me off at the hotel?"

"Sure, no problem."

The elevator doors swished shut and the car ascended towards her hotel floor. Brooke's phone buzzed a text alert. A glimmer of hope sparked at the thought that Jax might have sent her a message. Wishful thinking. He didn't have her number.

Brooke read the message. *Oh thank God.*

—*Sofia Rosso Baxter cleared of all charges in the case against Thurston Baxter.*—

The instant relief spurred tears to well. All she wanted to do was to seclude herself in the hotel room and sob out her pain. She stood in front of her door, key card in hand. Across the hall a door opened and Leo, a team member, emerged from his room rolling a suitcase.

"Hey Brooke, are you heading back to court this afternoon?"

"No. We're done. Originally I planned to stay a few days, but now I want to see if I can get on a flight early."

"I'm hitching a ride on the flight to the Dover base. I'm sure there's room for you."

"Thanks, but I'm heading back to Washington."

"Me, too. I really want to get back home. The baby is due any day. I'm renting a car once we land. It's only a two-hour drive. I wouldn't mind the company."

"I'd love a ride. I can't wait to get out of here. Just give me a few minutes to pack."

"I'll call and let them know you're coming with me."

"Thanks."

126

An hour later Brooke buckled into her seat on the military plane. The flight taxied to the runway, accelerated and lifted skyward taking her away from Jax forever.

Chapter 15

"Hey boss." Sergio waved a hand in front of Jax's face. "Yo. Good morning. I heard the news about Miss Sofia. What a relief. I'm so happy for you guys."

Jax blinked, focused on Sergio's smiling face and shook away the dark thoughts that had plagued him since the day before. Mom could put the nightmare behind her at last. He should be happy like Sergio—celebrating Mom's freedom. But his encounter with Brooke had left him miserable and wounded. He was still in love with the woman against all reason, but also angry, confused and bitter. How could he have given his heart to her when nothing about her was true? Yeah, Brooke was his dream girl all right. A total fantasy from start to finish.

Finished. That's what they were. He should have come to that conclusion when she had ghosted him weeks ago with her brother. Was Mike even her brother? Probably not. None of that mattered anyway. Nothing about Brooke James was real. *And I'm a real fool.*

"Yep. The nightmare's over, Serge." Was it really? Jax felt mired in a waking nightmare. "Is Mom here yet?"

"No." Sergio glanced at the watch on his wrist. "It's just about opening time. You better man the front."

Jax placed his hand on the swinging door, yet again deeply missing Brooke's sunny presence in the café despite his foolishness thinking about her at all. Would he ever stop missing her? He forced the go nowhere thinking to stop. She wasn't his waitress. She wasn't his anything. Brooke *Pellington* was an FBI Special Agent and the daughter of the formidable Director of the Agency himself. He had dived into surfing the net the night before to learn that tidbit.

Her presence in Pops' Café had opened the door for her to worm her way into his life and his heart. She had completely invaded his privacy secretly surveilling him and his mother. He couldn't believe he could be so stupid.

"I'll bet Mom is getting some extra sleep this morning. She deserves it. Let's do this, Sergio."

"I've got your back, man."

He flashed his cook a smile, shoved the door open and strode out into the restaurant.

The regulars stampeded into the place the minute Jax unlocked the front door. The best thing about those folks was that he didn't have to act "the host" for them on any day. Their seating was as established as their daily breakfast preferences. He didn't ask for their orders—just confirmed their "usuals" and got Sergio to work at the grill.

Thankfully the questioning about Brooke's absence had stopped weeks ago. That day everybody wanted to know why Sofia wasn't there. The morning rush required Jax's energy and concentration. But even his busyness couldn't distract him from growing more worried when his mother didn't appear. He couldn't wait to close for the day so he could go check on her.

The appearance of Hunter and Peggy at the front desk brightened Jax's mood. "Hey, guys. I'm glad to see you. I can't remember the last time you came for breakfast."

Peggy touched his sleeve. "Actually we came to give Sofia a big hug. She must be so relieved. Where is she?"

"Yesterday took a lot out of her," Jax said. "I thought I'd let her sleep in."

"Good idea." Peggy graced him with a broad smile. "Hunter, honey. I'll treat you to breakfast."

"I'll gladly eat with you, Ma, but my treat."

"Where would you like to sit?" Jax said.

"How about the booth by that window there." Peggy pointed to the table that Jax had come to think of as Brooke's and Mike's.

The memory of her beautiful face smiling at him the day he had met her jabbed him in the heart again. He sincerely wished he could force amnesia where she was concerned.

"The booth is yours." Jax picked up a couple of menus.

Peggy waved the menus away. "No need, honey. Two Pops' Specials. Right Hunter?"

"Yep."

But hold the bacon. Bacon always makes my sister fart. Ha, ha, Mike whoever you are. Apparently, their joke was on Jax.

He tamped down reminiscing about Brooke's stint in his life and chose instead to think about Pops as he went about the work of hosting and serving his grandfather's beloved customers. Jax would get over Brooke's deception eventually. His mother was free. That was all that mattered.

Hunter gave him a wave, and he sauntered over to the booth. His friend handed him his cell phone. "Have you seen this yet? Big news."

"What?"

"Read that headline."

Jax bent his head over the cell phone's screen scanning the news Ap's headlines until he found what Hunter surely wanted him to notice. "Thurston Baxter, CEO of Mercury Labs indicted for Espionage by a Federal Grand Jury."

His mind reeled. So Brooke and Mike had brought this about. And it followed that they had also had a hand in freeing his mother. Maybe that good deed would soften his opinion of Brooke eventually. But it didn't change anything really. Other than Baxter would probably be out of his mother's and his lives permanently—a very good development for Jax who didn't share Mom's opinion that her husband was innocent. He easily could see Baxter selling secrets to the Chinese and hauling in covert millions.

Jax hoped that Sofia hadn't seen the headline. She wouldn't view the indictment as good news—unlike her son.

He handed the phone back to Hunter. "I hope Mom is still sleeping and she hasn't read about this."

"Me, too." Peggy wiped her lips with a napkin. "Want me to go check on her?"

"No need," Jax said. "I'll head over to her house in an hour or so when I'm done here. I know she'll be very upset. She truly believes he's innocent."

"Do you think your stepfather's innocent?" Hunter said.

"Not for a second. And please don't call him that. He's not my anything." Jax smiled at Hunter to soften the slap down.

"Gotcha. Sorry man."

"No problem. Anything else I can bring you?"

Neither Peggy nor Hunter had requests, so Jax continued serving and clearing tables until the rush thinned out and gratefully ended. He couldn't wait to lock the door behind him so that he could go hold his mom's hand when she learned about what her husband faced.

Jax punched in the code at the security gates fronting the meandering, tree-lined drive up to the museum-like Baxter mansion. Pocketing his car keys and then mounting the steps to the front door of the "castle," Jax wondered if Sofia would move out of the place. The money from selling the monstrosity would surely provide a more than comfortable retirement. Could she divorce Baxter and claim the house? That proposition made him happy for the first time that day.

He rang the doorbell wagging his head at the sound of churchy chimes from within—pure pretention. As usual the stiffly formal butler opened the door and referred to him maddeningly as Master Jaxson in welcome.

"Uh, hello…" Jax strained to remember the man's name but came up empty.

He stepped into the vestibule. "Where would I find my mother?"

"I believe she's still resting in her room after her ordeal yesterday."

"Thanks." Jax was familiar enough with the place to know where his mother's room was—without using a map.

Mounting the stairs he mused about the fate of butler guy, whatever his name was, and the rest of the servants who resided somewhere in the place. Far as he knew, they were only loyal to Baxter. And who would pay them? He'd do anything for his mom short of financing anything that had to do with Baxter.

At Mom's closed bedroom double doors, Jax paused, conflicted about disturbing her and delivering the devastating news. He pushed down on the door handle inch by inch noiselessly and opened the door. The drapes were drawn, and the light was dim inside. Sofia's small body made a tiny mound under the covers in the massive, canopied bed.

"Mom?" he said softly tiptoeing into the room.

She didn't stir.

"Ma," he said louder nearing the bed.

No answer.

Alarm bells clanged inside Jax's head. "Ma!" He rushed forward and leaned over his sleeping mother. She lay on her side, one arm outstretched, with her mouth open. Her unnatural pose terrified him.

Clamping both hands on her shoulders he shook her body which did nothing to rouse her.

Scared senseless, Jax put his hand in front of her open mouth. No breath warmed him. Panicked, he laid his ear on her chest over her heart. No heartbeats registered thuds in his ear. He threw back the covers, rolled her on to her back, straddled her body and began administering CPR.

"Help! Somebody! Help!"

Afraid to stop compressions, he still sacrificed a few moments to dig out his cell phone from his pocket and to place the 911 call on speaker resuming CPR after he had dialed.

Jax heard the other bedroom door unlatch.

Somebody switched on the lights in the room. "Oh my God," came a female voice from behind him.

"I've called the paramedics." Jax didn't turn his head or stop compressions. "Let them in and bring them up here."

It seemed time had stopped and had suspended Jax in the unreality of working to revive his lifeless mother. Stomping feet preceded the feel of large hands on his shoulders. "We've got her, sir."

Jax allowed the paramedic to help him off the bed and set him on shaky, cramped legs. The EMTs surrounded his mother. "Clear."

The bed jerked as his mother's body was jolted with electricity. Jax took a few steps back, unable to stand the sight of her in mortal danger.

His eyes lit on a pill bottle on the bedside table. The cap was off, and the container lay on its side. Small pills scattered the surface of the table. He scooped it up and checked the label.

"What do you have there?" one of the EMTs said.

Jax squinted at the small print. "Nitroglycerin. Mom had a heart attack a little over a month ago."

The man turned to his team. "Let's get her into the truck."

Jax stood shaking while he watched the surreal tableau unfold. The paramedics lifted his mother's inert body onto a stretcher, rolled her out of her bedroom down the hall, folded the legs of the stretcher, carried her down the stairs and out the door on the run as Jax numbly trailed behind them.

Outside on the driveway they loaded the stretcher into the emergency vehicle and screeched away down the long, winding private road.

Jax jumped into his car and sped behind the truck. He gripped the steering wheel as if he could prevent himself from falling apart if he just squeezed tightly enough.

"Please, please, dear Lord, help her. Save her." He drove behind the truck with lights flashing and sirens blaring to the hospital, his thoughts colliding in his skull.

Had Mom read about her husband's indictment for Espionage? If she had, she had to know that he'd never leave prison if convicted. Or maybe he'd even receive the death penalty. That possibility might easily have caused another heart attack, if that's what she had suffered.

Jax knew that she loved Thurston Baxter, although Jax would never understand why. Maybe the guy was different behind closed doors even though he notoriously was painted negatively by anyone unfortunate enough to wind up in his orbit. How lonely could Mom have possibly been to cling to marriage with a man like him?

He followed the truck into the ambulance bay, switched off the engine and ditched the car right there not caring if they gave him a hundred tickets.

The doors of the ambulance were flung open, and his mother's stretcher was slipped out of the truck and propped on its rolling legs in seconds. A flurry of medical personnel raced through automatic doors, surrounded the stretcher and wheeled Mom inside the ER on the run.

Ultimately their urgency didn't matter. An hour later a doctor, clad in a powder blue coat sought Jax out in the waiting room. Although they had done their best to revive her, Sofia Baxter was dead.

Chapter 16

Jax slumped in the chair on his deck overlooking the ocean and rubbed his stiff neck. Spending the night in such an uncomfortable position dozing on and off might not have been the best decision but he couldn't face sleeping in the room he had shared with Brooke. The two days since his mother had died were a blur.

The plans were made for her funeral later that morning. Just the thought of the looming event made his heart skip a beat and tears track down his cheeks. He had played the "if only" game during his sleepless nights since her death.

If only he had stopped in to see his mom before work the day she died. Maybe he could have brought her to the hospital in time. Maybe he should have let Peggy go check on her when she offered.

If only he didn't go away to college. Maybe his mom wouldn't have married Baxter out of sheer loneliness.

If only he could turn back time.

His phone buzzed with a text from Hunter.

—*Hey buddy I'll be over in an hour. Do you need anything?*—

—*No I'm good. I'm going to shower. I'll leave the door open. Thanks for everything.*—

What would he have done without Hunter and his parents? Peggy had taken charge of phone calls and had insisted on having everyone back to Peggy's Place after the burial as a gift to Jax and her dear friend, Sofia. Hunter had accompanied Jax to the church to speak with Sofia's beloved priest, Father Santos Castillo aka Father Sunny who had agreed to officiate at her funeral Mass. Then Hunter had taken Jax to the funeral home where he had tried to make the horror of selecting a casket everyday—like just a quick shopping trip. Peggy had helped him pick out flowers.

Everything they did had attempted to convey to Jax that he wasn't alone.

He had never felt more alone in his life.

Jax stared out at the ocean, aching deep down in his bones…his heart…his soul. He forced his cramped body out of the chair and went back into the condo to prepare for the ceremony. The steaming hot water in the shower helped to loosen his stiff muscles. He wiped the fog off the mirror with a hand towel and then shaved.

I should have gotten a haircut.

He smiled despite his depression. Surely his mother had put that thought in his head.

His black suit hung in the back of his closet in a dry cleaner bag with a starched white shirt and a silver and black tie. The last time he had worn the suit was for Pops' funeral. He planned on throwing it away after his mother's.

The alarm double beeped signifying his front door opening.

"Hey buddy it's me," Hunter boomed.

"I'll be right out!" Jax finished tying his tie in the bathroom mirror and then strode into the great room.

He stopped dead in his tracks at the sight of Dryden, Bubba, Hunter and Ty, leaning against his kitchen counter. The Bama Boys came. For him. Their thoughtfulness was almost his undoing. His breath hitched and his throat clogged.

"I can't believe you guys are here. Thank you." Jax managed to speak over the lump in his throat.

The foursome hung over a huge tray of cookies on the counter. Jax smiled despite his barely contained tears. "Kamille's?"

Ty chuckled and gave Jax a nod. "Do you think Mama Kamille would let me come empty handed?"

Jax walked over to the counter and nabbed a chocolate coconut macadamia enjoying the richness of the treat and the happy memories of sharing in Ty's "care packages" of Kamille's Kookies in college.

"I still can't believe you guys are here," Jax said.

"Where else would we be?" Dryden said. "Our brother needs us today. So here we are." He emptied the contents of a brown shopping bag out onto the counter placing five shot glasses next to a bottle of Jose Cuervo. Dryden had started the tradition of meeting in the locker room the night before every game. Holding a tequila shot in hand the Bama Boys had declared, "Brothers forever. Let's kick their asses tomorrow."

Dryden filled the shot glasses, handed them out and then held his up. "Brothers forever…" He paused a moment. "For Mama Sofia."

Jax could barely swallow his shot. He was about to lay his Mama Sofia to rest. He'd never see her lovely face again or bask in her praise and love. He was grateful for the bolstering presence of his "brothers". *But oh, Ma. How I miss you.*

A stretch limousine idled in front of Jax's condo. The men piled inside. The sleek drive whisked them to the church. As if they had rehearsed, Dryden, Hunter, Ty and Bubba joined Jax as pall bearers of Sofia's casket at the back of the hearse.

Photographers milled like swarming gnats across the street from the church, shutters clicking rapidly. His mother's death was national news because of her association with Baxter. Jax seethed inside, but he ignored the photogs. He needed to focus on putting one foot in front of the other carrying his mother's casket down the long flower-scented aisle where Sofia's "village" filled the church to pay their respects to the finest woman Jax had ever known. How horrible that his mother was taken away from him. But how blessed he was that she was his.

Jax and the pall bearers gently placed the casket on the bier directly in front of the altar and then filed into the first pew to the left of the bier, Jax on the end so he could remain as close to his mother as possible. Hunter's parents were seated in the second row behind Jax. He turned to hug Peggy over the back of the pew and shook Hunter's dad's hand. He couldn't believe his eyes scanning the faces behind him. Coach Murphy, their Alabama baseball coach, sat next to Hunter's dad.

He leaned over and hugged Jax. "Anything you need, son. I'm here for you."

Jax could only nod as emotions swamped him. Seated in the pew, numb and hurting, he stared at his mother's casket in disbelief through the entire Mass. He stood when he needed to and knelt down when he needed to but not one word that Father Sunny said registered.

And then they carried her casket out of the church. And then he stood graveside for the final goodbye, his Bama Boys brothers at his side. Dryden had made the arrangements to close the cemetery for Sofia's funeral and only the limo and the hearse were allowed to enter through the gates. No photographers would interfere with his last moments with his mother. Dryden told Jax that he had directed his security team to try to stop the media from circulating any pictures of the day at all.

Father Sunny recited the prayers—*May your perpetual light shine upon her.* And then. It was over. The priest and his friends drifted away and left him alone with his mom. Jax stared at the flower-blanketed casket, finally allowing tears to fall. The day they had buried Pops, Jax's heart had broken. Standing there in almost the same spot in the same cemetery, Jax's heart shattered. He bowed his head. *Oh, Ma. I love you. Always.*

He composed himself and turned away from the grave. Jax tramped over the grass back to the car on wooden legs. A tornado of recriminations and regrets swirled inside. As they pulled away from the cemetery, Jax spotted a lone photographer standing on the other side of the gate holding a camera outfitted with a huge telephoto lens.

The parking lot at Peggy's Place was packed so the limo let them off in the street out front. Bubba put his arm around Jax and ushered him into the bar. The room was wall to wall people. Jax spotted regulars from Pops', barely recognizing Ed Kelly and his gents clad in suits and ties. It brought tears to his eyes at how many people truly loved his mom.

His brothers surrounded him. Bubba lightened the mood. "Let's get shitfaced."

****

Brooke bent at the waist with her hands on her hips panting after she had pushed her morning run. Her alarm didn't go off and she had overslept by half an hour. She caught her breath and bounded up her front stoop angling the Smartwatch on her wrist in front of her face to gauge how much time she had to get ready for the day and be on time for the breakfast date she had set with Mike the night before.

Mike Lynch was always on time.

He had returned from a weekend with Kay and as usual Kay had sent him home with some books that she thought Brooke just had to read. They had shared and recommended books to each other since they were little girls.

Brooke towel dried her hair and wound it into a bun on the top of her head. She donned an FBI blue hoodie and black leggings. She planned on spending the day in the office cleaning up files so there was no need for makeup. A quick glance in the mirror made her stop and rethink her "natural" face plans at her haggard appearance. There were dark circles under her eyes from lack of sleep.

Every time she closed her eyes she saw Jax's sweet mother's face. Sofia was so good to her for the short time she had worked at Pops' Cafe. How could she possibly be gone? Brooke wanted to reach out to Jax when she heard about his mother's death but after his reaction at the court house, she knew he would not appreciate a reminder of her part in the arrests that had very likely led up to Sofia's fatal heart attack. Her heart ached for him. According to the file, Baxter was denied release for his wife's burial leaving Jax totally alone. She could only hope that he preferred it that way.

Brooke tapped concealer under her eyes and swiped on a coat of pink lipstick before heading out the door.

Mike texted he was running late but was on his way. Not like him, but at least she had beaten him to her favorite breakfast spot. *After Pops Café, that is.*

Brooke nabbed a small booth and ordered coffee. She took a sip of the brew and checked the news on her phone. A headline about Sofia's funeral had her clicking through to the full article. Because of Thurston Baxter's indictment and upcoming trial, her funeral was national, maybe even international news. Two photos attached to the story. The first was a picture of Jax with four other men from behind lined up at her grave, all wearing funeral black suits. The caption read: The champion Bama Boys, Dryden Walker, Hunter Higdon, Ty Binder Martin, Will "Bubba" Walton and Jaxson Rosso. In the second picture Jax stood alone in profile, his eyes downcast and jaw clenched. Brooke's eyes filled with tears.

"Hey Pellington, long time no see." A tall muscular man with graying hair slid into the booth across from her.

She gave a start and dropped her phone in her lap.

"Sorry. I didn't mean to scare you."

"Still stealth-like, Gary." She grinned at him.

"Yeah. It's a gift. How's my favorite student? Are you ready to jump ship yet?"

Gary Stewart was one of her instructors at Quantico, had moved to the Secret Service and was promoted to Deputy Director. The day he was promoted he had contacted Brooke and had tried to recruit her to the Agency, but she wouldn't leave her father's command.

"I've thought about it lately," Brooke said.

"What? Are you kidding me? You can report tomorrow. This is great."

"Whoa. Slow down. I said I've given it some

thought. My father…"

"Yeah. He'll be pissed, so I won't pressure you right now. *But*. With the elections coming up we really need more female agents to protect the candidates, and you are my first choice. You always have been. Secret Service would be a perfect fit for you. You don't need the training program. You shined at Quantico. And your record as a Special Agent more than qualifies you. Let me give you my card."

Brooke chuckled. "No pressure, though…"

"Excuse me, miss?" He summoned the waitress. "May I please borrow your pen for a minute?"

The petite brunette complied with his request, and he wrote a phone number and email address on the back of a business card before returning the pen to the waitress. "Thanks."

Gary handed his card to Brooke. "My personal info is on the back. The position is yours whenever you choose to accept it. I sure hope that I hear from you soon."

"Thank you, Gary. It's nice to be wanted. I'll give you a call either way."

Her stealthy possible future employer disappeared as fast as he had appeared.

"Sorry I'm late." Mike scooted into the booth where Gary had sat a couple of minutes before. As expected, he plopped a shopping bag filled to the brim with books next to her.

"That's so nice. I'll text Kay later and thank her. How was your weekend?"

"It was interesting." He picked up the menu.

The waitress took their orders while Brooke itched to ask him what he meant.

"Is everything okay with you and Kay?"

"Kay and I are fine. Maybe even better than fine. I need to tell you about something else."

"Uh oh. This doesn't sound good." Brooke slumped in her seat. How much more stressful news could she take?

"It's good news. Remember Jake Collins?"

"Maybe."

"I went to school with him. He lives in Indianapolis now. Kay and I went out to dinner with him and his wife, Suzanne. He wants to bring me in as partner in his tech company. It would mean moving to Indy and leaving the FBI. But it's a great opportunity and Kay and I will finally live in the same town. Hell, in the same state." He gave her a broad grin, joy written all over his face. "And this way, when we're married, Kay doesn't have to leave Riley's Children Hospital for a job in a NICU in the Quantico area. She loves that place."

"This is wonderful for you both!" She leaned over the tabletop and gave him a hug. "I'm so happy for you." Brooke punched him in the arm. "You scared me."

"Ow." He grinned at her and rubbed his arm. "I loved working with you at the Agency and I'm going to miss you. I wanted you to be the first to know."

"Well. It's not like you'll never see me again. I'm going to be your sister-in-law in a few months. I'll come for visits. And we can spend the holidays together. You'll get sick of me."

"I promise you I won't get sick of you. You're welcome anytime."

The waitress delivered their breakfast orders. Brooke had a hard time swallowing the bacon remembering their first meal at Pops' Cafe. *Bacon always makes my sister fart.*

She forced a smile so that Mike wouldn't detect how sad she was inside.

He paid for breakfast. "Wish me luck. I'm off to hand in my two week notice to your father."

"I'll be right behind you. I'm heading to the office next."

"Want to ride with me?"

"No thanks. My car is parked outside. Good luck, brother."

"Thanks sis. See ya."

Brooke sat behind the wheel and watched Mike pull out of the parking spot ahead.

A life decision gelled. She dialed the number on the back of Gary's business card.

He answered on the first ring.

"Hi, Gary. What time do you want me there tomorrow?"

Chapter 17

The pounding would not stop. Was it the beer that Jax had chugged one after the other the night before, and every night for the past two weeks, until he had passed out? He wished he'd pass out again because the unremitting pounding hurt his ears as well as his head.

"Let me in or I'm calling the cops!"

"Go away," he mumbled.

He scrunched the pillow up over the sides of his head recognizing Hunter's booming voice. Muffling the yelling and banging didn't help much.

Jax groaned and rolled in slow motion into a sitting hunch on the edge of the bed. His head ached and spun, and his joints creaked in protest.

Bam, bam, bam!

"Yeah, yeah, I'm coming…"

Hunter couldn't possibly have heard Jax over his hammering on Jax's front door while he tossed out curses and threats.

By the time Jax limped out of his room and through his condo to let his friend in, Hunter had threatened everything that Jax held dear. Which wasn't much. Nothing was left for him.

He swung open the door and went on the offensive nose to nose with his furious friend. "What the hell is wrong with you? I should call the police on you for disturbing the peace."

"What's wrong with *me*? Are you effing kidding me? Just look at you."

Jax hadn't looked in a mirror in a couple weeks. He scrubbed a hand over his face and brow. Stubble had proliferated and his Biblical length hair was greasy. What did it matter?

"Do you have any headache pills by any chance? I ran out." Jax eyed Hunter dully.

"For god's sake, sit down," Hunter said. "I'll make some coffee."

"Yeah well." Jax held his ground slightly swaying on his feet. "I'm not in the mood for coffee. Or company."

Hunter brushed past him and marched into the kitchen. No one had ever made a pot of coffee more aggressively. Hunter's lips pursed in a disapproving, straight line. He slid a mug of brew over the counter.

Resigned that he couldn't shake the intrusion immediately, Jax slid onto a stool, picked up the mug and took a sip. His stomach heaved, so he put the cup down not daring to meet his friend's eyes.

"I'm worried about you, Jax."

He had no response. Deep down Jax appreciated that somebody cared enough to worry about him. But as much as he valued his relationship with the Bama Boys, and Hunter in particular, no one could substitute for Pops or Mom...or Brooke.

Jax longed for his bed while he felt the heat of Hunter's glare blasted at him from across the kitchen counter.

"Look at me," Hunter growled.

Stalemate. Jax fixed his gaze on his lap.

"Please, look at me." Hunter's tone softened.

Might as well face him. Maybe then he'll leave me alone.

Jax met Hunter's penetrating gaze. The tenderness he detected in the brawny man's eyes undid him. "I'm sorry, Hunter," he slurred.

"Don't apologize to me…" Hunter's cell phone chirped diverting him from the anticipated lecture.

"Hey. Yeah, I'm with him." Hunter put the call on speaker and placed his cell phone on the counter between him and Jax. "Don't apologize. Just take this call."

"Hello?"

"Hey, Jax."

"Dryden?"

"The same. How are you doing?"

Jax heaved a sigh. "Just *dandy.*"

"I feel your pain, Jax. I do. We all miss Sofia."

He held his tongue. What good would it do to rail at his friend and proclaim his loss as monumental compared to his?

"Are you still there?"

"Yeah." *God my head hurts.*

"I want you to accept my offer," Dryden said.

"What offer?"

"You didn't tell him, Hunter?"

"Didn't get the chance yet. I thought I'd need a battering ram to get in here this morning."

Dryden hooted a laugh. "Oh. Okay. Jax I want you to accept the position of CFO of Walker Communications Industries. I know you'll like the compensation package. Full benefits. And residence in one of the company's condos on Michigan Avenue until you can find your own place."

"I…" Nothing Dryden had said made sense in Jax's

alcohol muddled mind. "Chicago?"

"Yeah, Chicago."

"But…"

"But what?" Hunter interjected. "Buddy, you are taking this job."

"What about the café? I can't just leave."

"Leave? What do you think you've done since Sofia's funeral? You've left Sergio entirely on his own. Do you really think Ed Kelly and my mom have nothing better to do than to volunteer to run your restaurant? While you lose yourself in a bottle of beer? Dryden, say something before I punch Jax's lights out."

"It's not my restaurant. It's my mom's." Jax's heart ached just uttering the word, mom.

"Which you inherited. Look, Jax. We want to help you get back on your feet. I'll make it as easy as I possibly can if you cooperate. There's nothing keeping you here. Except living near stellar friends like me and Lyn, that is," Hunter said.

"Moving to Chicago brings you near stellar friends like me and Joelle," Dryden said. "The windy city is beautiful. When it's not a polar vortex."

"Take the job," Hunter said. "Trust us."

A tiny chink of shining possibility broke through Jax's haze of grief. He might see his way forward as an orphan and a bachelor if he accepted Dryden's offer. He had visited Chicago a few times on business. Except for experiencing some world class restaurants, Jax mostly saw the inside of conference rooms. Weather in the Midwest was notoriously lousy but on a pretty, sunny day the Chicago riverfront and lakefront were picture perfect.

Jax could envision morning jogs along the Lake

Michigan shoreline, savoring deep dish pizza and walking city blocks below towering skyscrapers edging the sea-like lake. It wasn't the Pacific ocean and sunshine was hardly the norm like in Luna Beach, but he hadn't enjoyed much better weather than Chicago's living in New York City.

Why not?

"I don't know what to say, Dryden. Are you sure I'm the man for the job? I haven't exactly…"

"Stop right there. You're brilliant, Jax. I want brilliant people on my team. Simple as that. This isn't charity or buddy nepotism. If it didn't make business sense, I would never propose hiring you or anybody else."

"Okay…" Jax took the leap. "Thank you so much, Dry. What did you have in mind for a start date? I have to figure out things here. A mover…"

"The condo is furnished, Jax. So if you want to keep your place there or if it doesn't sell quickly or whatever, you don't have to worry about moving furniture. Hunter, have you figured out a plan yet to get Jax organized?"

"Yeah. My mom and I will go over it all with Jax today."

Jax felt powerless that others apparently had mapped out his future—and deeply grateful at the same time.

"Okay, then," Dryden said. "You know how to reach me, Jax, when you're ready to move on this. Call my office and they'll arrange the flight for you on the corporate jet. See you soon. Bye guys."

The phone connection dropped. Hunter pocketed the cell phone and leaned on the counter, too close to Jax's face. "You smell. Go shower and shave. My barber is expecting you in an hour. And then we're going to Pops' Café. Move, Jax."

Jax narrowed his eyes at the surge of opposition that arose inside him in reaction to Hunter's ordering him around. But he held his tongue knowing that if he resisted following direction, the Bama Boys would hound him mercilessly.

Hunter hung over the refrigerator door and grimaced. "Nothing edible in here. Eat when you get to Pops'."

He banged closed the fridge door, turned around, folded his arms, and faced Jax.

Nothing left to do but to go through the motions and comply with his friend's forceful bidding. The shower helped clear a modicum of hangover fog. His electric razor worked overtime until his face was smooth shaven again. He eyed his reflection in the mirror thinking about how Sofia would view his hair length—a disgrace. A shave and a shower left him nowhere near shaking away his funk, but he had taken a couple steps in the right direction.

I'm not going to disgrace you anymore, Ma. He resolved to make his mother proud instead.

Jax had formulated a rudimentary plan without Hunter's input during the time between sitting in a barber chair and his friend's leaving him off at Pops' Café. He strode into the restaurant and headed to the kitchen well after the breakfast rush had cleared.

"Hey, Sergio."

His cook wiped his hands on his apron and held a hand out to Jax for a shake. "It's good to see you, boss."

Jax shook Sergio's hand. "You done for the day?"

"Miss Peggy said there's no more customers out

there when she left a half hour ago. So yes. Unless you want me to fix you something."

"How about I fix us both something and we talk for a bit. Do you have time?"

"Are you sure? I can…"

"I'm sure. Go sit down. I'll be right out."

"Okay. If you say so." He took off his apron, hung it on a peg on the wall and left his post behind the grill.

"Before I forget…" He halted with one hand on the swinging door. "Chuck Roberts stopped by earlier. He wants you to give him a call."

"Got it." Jax fired up the grill and fixed two Specials while his hollow stomach growled fiercely at the smell of fried eggs and bacon.

Seated across from Sergio, Jax laid out his plan. "If you're willing, the café is yours."

Sergio's eyes widened. "What the heck do you mean, boss?"

"I mean the place is yours. I inherited it from Mom, and I want to give it to you."

"But…I'm just the cook. I don't know anything about running a restaurant. Although…"

"Yeah?"

"I do have some ideas for the menu."

"You see? You've already thought about this. Maybe it's Pops channeling through you. You can hire help. I'll continue to subsidize your operating costs monthly until the day you're profitable."

"You're not profitable now?"

Jax chuckled. "Nope. No matter what Mom did, she couldn't build the customer base enough to compensate for higher cost of ingredients and fixed overhead. Because she didn't want to raise prices on her loyal regulars. You're free to make any changes you see fit. Pops would want it this way."

"Man. I don't know what to say. How long will you help the place financially?"

"Indefinitely. Pops would want it this way, too."

"This will mean so much to my family. Your kindness is overwhelming. I'm honored." He clasped Jax's hand over the table and pumped the handshake up and down.

For the first time in weeks a swell of satisfaction filled Jax. He wanted to move forward with kindness. Maybe he could.

"When I talk with Chuck I'll ask him to draw up whatever paperwork is necessary to make the transfer of ownership legal. But starting now, you own the show. I think you need to give some thought to hiring a waiter and possibly a host or hostess." Giving the simple advice shot a couple of arrows into Jax's heart.

Brooke, Ma. He doubted that he'd ever shake the sorrow of losing them.

However, when he left Sergio after they finished breakfast together, he felt lighter and more optimistic than he had since the horrible days when he had faced Brooke's subterfuge and then found his mother gone forever from him.

Amazing what filling your belly with his grandfather's favorite breakfast offering could do for a man. Ready to formalize the restaurant ownership, he dialed his mother's lawyer via the Bluetooth connection in his car.

Jax waited while Chuck's secretary put through the call.

"Jax. Good to talk with you."

"Same here, Chuck. I just left Sergio at Pops' Café. I'd like you to do what you do to make the restaurant officially his."

"Happy to. What's the purchase price?"

"I'm giving it to him. So maybe all I have to do is sign some papers or something?"

"I'll draw up the docs."

"Not to rush you, but sooner rather than later, okay? I just accepted a position in Chicago, and I think it would do me good to leave as soon as possible."

"I understand. Since you're leaving I expect you want to sell the real estate."

"You mean Pops' condo that I inherited? No. I'm keeping it. At least for now."

"I'm sorry I wasn't clear. I mean the house you inherited from your mother."

"My mom? You mean the Baxter castle? I can't see Baxter standing still for that. Anyway, isn't the house all tied up with the indictment and all that?"

"Bank accounts, including your mother's, were frozen by the government. But the house was never deeded to Thurston Baxter. Only to your mother. So it's part of her estate and you're the sole heir."

The information hit him like an electric shock. "You mean the guy was actually generous to my mother in the long run?"

Chuck burst out laughing. "Maybe by default. I think he was distancing himself from connecting assets to ill-gotten gains. Anyway, I had the house appraised during probate. Should I list it for you?"

He pulled into his garage and cut the engine. "Yeah, sure."

"I'll get everything to you via online signature

services. Based on the market analysis, I suggest you set the list price at $20 million."

"Holy shit."

Chapter 18

Three Months Later

The frigid wind blew Jax's coat collar up against his neck. No doubt about it, winter in Chicago wasn't for sissies. The Christmas countdown was at seven days, and the streets were clogged with shoppers. Just the thought of Christmas this year twisted Jax's stomach in knots. Last year at that time his mom had visited him in New York City. Her detestable husband had a business trip and Sandra was away visiting family. Jax had convinced Sofia to accept a first-class airline ticket and to stay for a week in his guest room while he spoiled her. He had taken off work so they could spend their time together sightseeing.

She had marveled at the famous Rockefeller Center tree adorned with Christmas lights. They had sipped hot chocolate and watched the ice skaters on the rink below the tree. Sofia had delighted in window shopping along 5th Avenue. When she had admired a dress in one of the windows, Jax had ushered her into the store and had refused to leave until she had tried on the dress. He had bought it for her for Christmas. They had finished the visit with tickets to the Radio City Music Hall show with the Rockettes. Saying good bye to Sofia at the airport was hard afterward. It was unbelievable to Jax that less than a year later he had said goodbye to her for good.

Jax shoved his grief and sadness deep down inside where it always resided and kept moving forward. He needed to stop at the wine shop to pick up a special bottle of wine for Dryden who would host the annual company Christmas party that night. He would rather do anything than go to a party, but attendance was mandatory for all healthy employees. Besides, he owed Dryden everything for helping him to get his life back together. Jax loved the new job and was starting to feel at home in Chicago.

As usual, the line at the Garrett's popcorn store snaked outside in the polar air. Despite a likely long wait no matter when he joined the line, he'd stop on the way back to his condo after buying a bottle of wine. Dryden's girlfriend, Joelle, had two sons and Jax was sure they would love some of the famous Chicago cheese and caramel mix. He'd pick up a can of chocolate drizzle for himself, too. The stuff was addictive.

He had done his Christmas shopping on line. When he lived in New York he had sent everyone on his list an assortment of pastries from his favorite shop in the city—*Zabar's* had the best croissants and rugclach. Jax liked the thought of gifting Christmas morning breakfast to all his friends, so this year he continued the tradition. He sent some to himself, too. The Bears would play on Christmas Day, and Jax planned to root for his now favorite team while devouring rugelach and decadent popcorn.

A light snow fell by the time he had finished shopping and pushed through the revolving door of his building. His mother's estate had settled, and the mansion had sold for an obscene price in Jax's estimation. He needed to think about getting his own place in the new year. He planned to speak with Dryden about purchasing a condo in that fabled building where the company condo was located. Jax could afford to live in the penthouse. Even with it's likely huge price tag, he still would have the majority of the proceeds of the sale of the mansion left to invest. But he was too careful with his money to throw it away on prestige. The most modest properties in the building were still pretty impressive.

After an elevator ride up to the fortieth floor, Jax approached the door to his unit. Two boxes leaned against the wall to the right of the entry. He lugged an oversized box inside first and then he hefted the other box into his arms, stepped inside, and closed the door behind him.

A note inside the larger of the two boxes read:

Hi Jax! Everyone needs a Christmas tree. We expect a photo as soon as you have finished decorating. We love you. Sending hugs, Lyndsey (and Hunter who says the hugs are from me not him.)

The large box contained a live, three-foot tall pine tree. Visions of stabbing his bare feet with pine needles abounded. He groaned after he had opened the second box which predictably contained ornaments and lights with a timer included. Stringing lights on the tree was the bane of his holiday traditions with his mother. Hanging ornaments was only slightly less drudgery. He had liked picking out the tree at the choose-and-cut farm every year, but he had unapologetically left the rest to her once he was adult enough to protest.

But he couldn't disappoint his closest friends when they had gone to so much trouble to brighten the season for him. He carried the tree into his living room, secured it in the stand that Hunter and Lyndsey had had the foresight to provide, and positioned it in the center of the wall of floor to ceiling windows.

Might as well get this over with...

Jax strung the lights and then plugged them in. His mood brightened when they all lit up. He hung the ornaments and then stepped back with his phone in hand to provide Lyn with proof that he had used her gift as directed.

He grinned as he focused through the view finder. The sparkling little tree looked pretty with the backdrop of falling snow on the cityscape through his window. Jax texted the photo and a heartfelt thank you to her and then sat down at his desk to catch up on some work.

At sunset, he leaned back in the chair and gazed at the tree. It looked even prettier in the gathering darkness and made his temporary home come alive with Christmas spirit. Jax rose from his seat and headed to the shower.

Dress, per the invitation, was holiday themed, business formal so Jax chose to wear a starched red and white striped shirt tucked into black dress pants and a pine green cashmere vee neck sweater.

The drive to the Walker Communications Industries building only took five minutes. Jax usually walked to work, but toting a bottle of wine and cans of popcorn exposed to the biting wind and falling snow didn't appeal. He pulled into his reserved parking space in the garage and rode the employee elevator to the executive suite on the top floor. The elevator doors swished open revealing the transformation of the large conference room and reception area into a winter wonderland of twinkling lights hanging from the ceiling and three huge glimmering trees that framed the windows which overlooked a sweeping view of Lake Michigan.

Dryden and Joelle stood near the elevator greeting their guests. They beamed as Jax approached them.

"Wow. The place looks great, Dry." Jax handed him the bottle of wine.

"I didn't have anything to do with it. It's all Joelle." Dryden drew the petite blonde into a side hug.

"Great job, Joelle," Jax said.

"I guess I went a little overboard. But when I asked Dryden about the budget and he said whatever I needed, well, a million fairy lights it was."

"I brought something for the boys." Jax held up the cans of popcorn. "Are they here?"

"They're hiding out in Dryden's office elated with unrestricted screen time. They're gonna love this treat. Thanks, Jax."

A chatty group exited the elevator cuing Jax to move away from the hosts. "I'll deliver this popcorn to the boys and catch up with you guys later."

Jax shook hands and kissed cheeks on the way to Dryden's apartment-sized office. Joelle's kids, Jason and Jeff, sat side by side on the couch in front of a mammoth TV screen pounding on video game controllers.

Jason spotted Jax first. "Wanna play?"

"I wish I could, but I have to go back to the party. I just wanted to give you guys these." He handed each a can.

Jeff paused the game. He and Jason popped the lids off the cans, grabbed a handful of the popcorn and stuffed their mouths. The buttery smell of caramel and cheese popcorn had Jax digging in when Jeff offered to share. He sat down on the couch, munched popcorn and watched them resume playing their game. The boys didn't seem to notice when he left the room to join the party.

A string quartet played Christmas music adding a note of elegance. Jax paced over to the buffet table, picked up a dinner plate and took a place in line.

"Well, there goes my diet," a female voice that seemed familiar came from behind him.

He turned around and his eyes widened. Her voice *was* familiar from TV coverage of the November election. Vice President Elect Grace Burrows smiled at Jax.

"You don't need a diet." Jax handed her a plate and relinquished his position in line to her, doing his best to hide how starstruck he was.

She looked much younger in person than when he had seen her on the news a few days before. He was drawn to her shining, sea blue eyes and radiant smile.

"Exactly what a girl wants to hear." She grinned and extended her hand. "Grace Burrows."

Jax clasped her hand gently. "Of course I know who you are. I voted for you."

"I like a man who is smart *and* handsome." She left her hand in his and gazed directly at him, her eyes dancing.

"Exactly what a man wants to hear." He released her hand. "I'm Jaxson Rosso. My friends call me Jax. It's truly an honor to meet you Madam Vice President."

"My friends call me Grace."

Their eyes locked and for the first time in months Jax felt a shimmer of attraction. "Grace it is. I'm starving. How about you?"

"Famished."

She walked at his side down the buffet line putting food on his plate and allowing him to put food on hers.

"Let's find somewhere quiet to eat all this." Grace scanned the packed room. "If that's even possible."

"I know just the place." He took her by the hand.

"On this floor?" she said.

Jax pointed to his left. "Yes. Just down that hallway."

She turned her attention to a burly man with an ear piece who stood by the elevator bank. "I'll be back in little while, Brad. Why don't you make yourself a plate and enjoy the party?"

Brad nodded but didn't budge an inch from his post.

Grace stood in the office doorway while Jax switched on his desk lamp. "Are you sure it's okay to be in here?"

"Yes. It's my office." Jax pulled out one of two upholstered chairs in front of his desk for her.

She placed her plate on the edge of his desk and took her seat gazing at her surroundings.

Jax sat down on the chair next to her.

Grace pointed to a framed photo on the wall. "Dryden has the same picture in his office. He told me once that it was his college field." She took a bite of a lobster-tail-sized shrimp. "Did you play baseball with Dryden?"

"I did. I met him my freshman year. How did you meet him?"

"We're from the same home town. Before he was elected to Congress, my dad coached Dryden in little league. And then he followed Dryden all through high school. He always said, 'That boy is something.'

"When Congress wasn't in session, Dad came home and caught as many of his games as he could. After Dad had his first stroke, Dryden's high school won the state championship and Dryden stopped at our house to give my dad his game ball. It meant the world to him."

"I'm not surprised. Dryden is one of the most caring people I have ever met in my life. I'm honored to call him a brother." Jax balled up his napkin and tossed it into his trash can. "I didn't want to come to this party. Dry insisted. Now I'm so thankful that he did." Jax looked into Grace's eyes. "I hope we can see each other again even though you'll be pretty busy the next four years." He gave her a crooked grin.

Her eyes lit with her wide smile. "I would like that." She leaned back in her chair and sighed. "I can't eat another bite."

"Did you see that coconut cake on the dessert table?" Jax teased.

"Oh, you are a wicked boy, aren't you?"

"I try." He stood, picked up their plates and ushered her out of his office encountering Dryden in the hallway.

"The food was delicious, Dryden. I'm having the best time." Grace winked at Jax.

"We tried a new caterer this year. Glad you liked it, Grace. I've been hunting down Joelle. Have you seen her?"

"Sorry no. We ate in my office. Now we're going to get some dessert," Jax said.

"Try the coconut cake. It's great. I've had two pieces already. I think I see Joelle. Let me know if you need anything." He scurried away.

Grace burst out laughing. "Now we *have* to try the cake."

They avoided some calories by sharing a delicious piece of cake before Grace declared it was time for her to leave. But she gave him her personal phone number and accepted his before beckoning her security guard.

Jax made the rounds of the party before slipping away, too.

The temperature must have dropped twenty degrees, and it took longer than the ride home for the heat in his truck to actually warm him.

He parked in the garage of his condo building, cut the engine and rested his hands on the steering wheel. Grace was a special lady. He had enjoyed himself in her company and realized that for the last four hours he hadn't thought about Brooke once.

Maybe he was finally ready to let Brooke go and move on.

Chapter 19

Jax stretched out his long legs, propped them up on the coffee table and crossed his ankles. He wielded the TV's remote control like a sword, jabbing it in the direction of the screen with each channel change. Nothing interested him on network or cable. Maybe watch a movie?

Nah. New Year's Rockin' Eve it is.

He switched to the broadcast and viewed the familiar chaos in Times Square: shoulder to shoulder humanity who essentially were imprisoned on the spots they had staked out earlier in the day after security scrutiny and clearance. Ever since the attack on the World Trade Center the event was strictly controlled on New Year's Eve. Once you were permitted into the area around the ball drop you stayed put until after the new year rang in. Jax figured that the sales of adult diapers skyrocketed in NYC around that time. Glad that he could watch the ball drop from the comfort of his warm condo, he relaxed on the sectional.

Jax remembered the storied New Year's Eve event in more innocent times when he was in college. The Bama Boys and their dates had cut short their winter break at home and traveled to New York City before returning to school for the start of second semester. Their budgets hadn't allowed much luxury in the big city, but gawking at the tree in Rockefeller Center and standing in

Times Square for the new year's countdown was gloriously free. There were no restrictions on access to the ball drop area. Plus you could see the giant illuminated ornament hanging from the flagpole at One Times Square from any number of feeder streets. More or less warmed by bulky winter coats and too many beers earlier, Jax had wholeheartedly kissed his date and any other willing lady in his vicinity when the ball hit bottom. He was glad that he had experienced the scene when he was younger and much more stupid.

But alone on his couch watching from afar with no one to kiss or care wasn't exactly Jax's idea of a life improvement. During the past couple weeks Jax just wanted the holiday season to be over. Exhibiting cheer and good will drained him. He missed Sofia terribly. Pops, too. But most of all, he missed Brooke. He had debated calling Grace, but in the end had decided not to. Why start something with the lady when she would leave for Washington in less than three weeks to work there for a minimum of four years? Jax had had enough of women leaving him.

At least the time difference between the East Coast and Chicago would end that dismal year for Jax at eleven p.m. He could go to bed and hopefully start a better life in the morning. Light taps on his door sounded, rousing Jax from his inertia in front of the TV. He rose from the couch and strode to the door slipping his credit card and a ten dollar bill out of his wallet to pay for and tip the pizza delivery driver. Lou Malnati's pizza would go a long way to salvage his evening.

But when he swung open the door, instead of his late dinner delivery, he encountered Grace Burrows toting a bottle of champagne, barefoot and dressed in sweats.

She gave him a sheepish grin and held out the bottle in his direction. "I just took this off ice and thought how sad to drink it alone. Want to share it with me?"

Her appearance there, especially without shoes on her feet, was so improbable to Jax that for a second he was struck dumb.

Grace knit her brow and turned slightly as if positioning to run. "I should have called. I'll leave."

Jax reached out a hand and touched her arm. "No, please. I was just expecting someone else."

A high blush reddened her porcelain skin. "Oh my, that's worse. I'm sorry to barge in."

He stepped out into the hallway and put an arm around her shoulder. "I'm botching this something awful. Please come in, Grace. And when the person I'm expecting—the Lou Malnati's delivery guy—appears you can share dinner with me."

"Ah. Okay. That sounds good." She allowed him to usher her inside and close the door after he had looked up and down the hall.

"No giant bodyguard with you?"

Grace sidled up to his kitchen counter and placed the bottle of champagne atop the marble. "Brad's not exactly a bodyguard per se. He's on my Secret Service detail. He thinks I'm in my pj's on the couch and he, along with the rest of the detail are hopefully enjoying leisure time instead of worrying about me."

"I couldn't help but notice. Where are your shoes? And your coat for that matter?"

"I live two floors above you. The decision to knock on your door was pretty impromptu."

"I'm glad you came." He gave a head tilt toward the TV. "We can change that if you want."

She turned in the screen's direction. "No need. We can at least get a countdown out of it. Even though the new year comes an hour sooner."

Grace smiled at him. She really did have a lovely smile.

Jax ducked behind the counter, set out two champagne flutes, removed the foil and muselet from the bottle, wrapped a clean towel around the cork and then popped it. He expertly caught fizz in a flute, filled both glasses and handed one to Grace.

She held hers up towards him. "Cheers."

"Cheers." Jax took a sip. "Very good."

"Mmm. I agree. Shall we sit?"

He nodded, trailed her to the sofa and sat down next to Grace. She closed the distance between them and leaned her head against his shoulder. "I hope you don't mind."

"Not at all." Jax took another sip of champagne, put the glass on an end table to his left and then encircled her shoulders with his right arm.

She nestled her head in the crook of his neck and gazed at the TV. Her hair felt soft against his skin, and she smelled lovely—expensive.

"Ever been there?" Grace said.

"Yes. Years ago. When you didn't have to worry about having to pee."

Grace hooted a laugh. "It kind of looks like happy insanity even so."

The emcee's voice droned introducing a band who played a song Jax had never heard before. He had never heard of the band, either, for that matter. When did he get so unhip and out of touch?

"Tell me about you." Grace's soft voice was almost

drowned out by the music.

"Hang on." He leaned forward, reached for the remote, tapped mute and then repositioned on the couch drawing Grace back to cuddle next to him.

"What would you like to know, Grace?"

"Anything and everything. So you played championship baseball with Dryden. What else should I know about you? Ever married?"

The image of Brooke's beautiful face flashed in his mind. He would have married her in an instant. "I've come close, but no. You were, of course. Your bio was splashed everywhere during your campaign."

She looked up at him. There was no mistaking the sadness swimming in her eyes. "My husband was my hero in every sense of the word. He was a patriot, something my dad, who was serving in Congress when I started dating Joe, approved of enormously. Dad instilled a deep desire in me to be of service to my country. There was no question, to him at least, that I would win his Congressional seat when he had to vacate it because of his stroke. But Joe? His sacrifices in military service were far greater than us Congressmen. His death during the Afghanistan withdrawal shattered me, Jax."

"Having recently been shattered by losing a loved one, I completely understand."

"Your mom?"

No need to mention Brooke, even though in some ways, her loss was even more shattering to Jax. "Yes. I suppose you know the details. My stepfather's treason made national news."

"Uh huh." She nodded. "I received several security briefings on him. I'm so sorry for what it did to your mother."

"Thanks." Jax had to change the subject. Wallowing in grief with company felt worse than wallowing alone. "So…no Second Gentleman candidates on the horizon for you?"

"Lord, no. I've hardly had time to think during this crazy campaign. It didn't leave room for a love life, that's for sure. Are you dating anybody, Jax?"

"Not since I left New York." Maybe he could finally forget about Brooke if he erased her from his life story. "Sandra and I were living together when my mother had a heart attack. I'm an only child and my dad deserted her before I was born. I couldn't get back to California fast enough to help her recuperate. My granddad was like a father to me, and he took wonderful care of my mother when I left for college. But by the time Mom had the heart attack, he had passed away and left the little café he owned to her. I used to work at the café when I was a kid, so I knew the ropes. I wanted to help her keep the place open until she was strong enough to manage it herself."

"What about your stepfather? Couldn't he pitch in to help her?"

Jax snorted. "You mean her crooked husband? Frankly, he was a self-centered prick who didn't deserve her in the least. Totally selfish. And apparently a criminal to boot. It would have been nice if he used all the money for *some* good purpose like helping his wife. But he didn't give her a dime. Rotting in jail forever is more than he deserves."

"How do you *really* feel, Jax?" Her eyes danced.

They burst out laughing. "Well…" Jax recaptured his breath. "The only good thing he ever did for her, in my opinion, is exonerate her from his wrong doing.

Thank God the Grand Jury believed her. In the end…"

"I think your story about Sandra kind of got lost there," she interjected.

"Right. She accused me of being a mama's boy and declared that if I chose to run to Sofia's aid, she wouldn't be there when I returned. She wasn't."

"Ouch. That's harsh. So have you sworn off women?"

That might make his life considerably easier. "No." He grinned at her taking in her parted lips and the knowing gleam in her eye.

He was definitely attracted to Grace. Who wouldn't be? She was pretty and athletic and brilliant, not to mention second in power to the most powerful man in the world. Her dad was a legend for his diplomacy and fairness and untiring dedication to work in the best interests of his constituents. There was never even a whiff of scandal in her dad's history and his daughter was no different.

Jax was flattered that she trusted him enough to sit there alone with him without her bodyguard's threatening presence. He could kiss her. He should kiss her.

The doorbell rang and they both jumped in their seats.

Grace put a hand over her heart. "Good grief that scared me to death."

"You like pizza?" Jax rose from the couch.

"Sure, who doesn't?"

He gave her a half smile. "Then, you'll want me to answer the door."

Jax accepted the delivery and brought the pizza box and small bag containing paper plates and napkins over to the coffee table, his hand warm on the bottom of the cardboard. He handed Grace the bag and she dug inside and "set" the table. Jax placed the box between their two paper plates and opened it. The savory fragrance of a Lou Malnati's Special: four cheeses, spinach and thin tomato slices covered with a blanket of parmesan cheese had his mouth watering.

"Yum." She grabbed a slice, folded it in half and took a not so delicate bite.

Her face alight with pleasure, Grace scarfed the entire slice down before he could swallow his first sampling. She reached for another. Holding her plate beneath the gooey meal, she settled back against the sofa cushions.

"I can't believe I'm this hungry. I ate a full dinner and everything. But yum. Thanks for having the foresight to order a large. Did you somehow know that I'd pay you a visit tonight?"

Biggest surprise of the last three months. "I didn't. But I'm very glad you're here. I typically order a large so I can freeze half for another meal."

Grace chewed unceremoniously. She seemed like she was having tremendous fun. She seemed like tremendous fun in general. "I love to cook, and I've been told I'm very good at it. I'll have to make you dinner before I leave for Washington."

Of course she'd leave. But she wasn't disappearing without a trace. He'd know exactly where she was— probably more than any other woman because of her position. Washington wasn't that far from Chicago. Heck, with his inheritance he could probably buy a plane. Or maybe she'd send Air Force 2 for him. He wouldn't hold back. If she was interested, he'd give the relationship a chance.

"My gosh, it's almost eleven o'clock," she said.

"Time for our not really the new year here countdown."

Jax picked up the remote and unmuted the audio. The crowd in New York were in a frenzy. The camera panned the famous square and then fixed the focus on the ball high atop the building.

Ten, nine...

The Waterford crystal ball shuddered a little and began its descent.

Three, two...

As if choreographed, Grace and Jax put down their plates.

One!

He took her in his arms and kissed her. If he held Brooke, he would have deepened the kiss, squeezed harder in the embrace. If Grace were Brooke, she'd kiss him fiercely back, press herself harder against his chest. The kiss that Grace and Jax exchanged was sweet and beyond a friendly peck. She didn't press her body against his. She didn't part her lips for him. Maybe they hadn't known each other long enough to kindle passion. Or maybe no matter how long they knew each other, they never would.

Jax liked her enormously, but they both deserved more than lukewarm kisses. He released her gently. She picked up her champagne flute and swigged some.

And then she gazed into his eyes. "I like you so much, Jax but..."

He took her hand, brought it to his lips and kissed it. "You're not looking for entanglements now that you won the election."

She twisted her lips and tilted her head. "Probably. Maybe I haven't stopped loving Joe with all my heart yet. You are *very* handsome, and I don't want to offend you."

"No offense taken. Thank you for the compliment, Grace. I like you, too." He was too much of a gentleman to tell her that he wasn't the least overcome with desire like he was when he had first kissed Brooke. Let the lady dump him if that was her intention.

"Friends?"

"Grace, I'd be honored to be your friend."

"I want to ask you something, but I'm afraid I'll offend you further."

"I've got a pretty thick skin. Ask away."

"Would you please be my escort at the Inauguration? I can't stand the thought of all that dancing at the balls with whomever they drum up for the dateless widow."

He chuckled. "First of all, I'd be honored, yes. Second of all, wow."

Her eyes gleamed. "All the parties really are something. I think we'd have fun."

"I know we would."

She put her champagne glass down on the coffee table. "Happy New Year, Jax. I'm so glad I met you."

"Happy New Year, Grace." Despite the lack of sparks between them, Jax thought that beginning the new year with her was perfect—and hopeful.

"Let me walk you to your condo?"

"I'd like that."

She fitted her key in the lock, opened the door, stepped inside and turned to face him.

"Good night, Grace."

"Night." She turned away and then stopped short. "Oh, wait. One more thing?"

"Yes?"

"I'm doing a little—well maybe not so little— appreciation gathering at the local coffee house tomorrow morning at ten. I did a lot of stumping there and those good folks supported me with their votes. Would you consider going with me? All the coffee you can drink and pastries you can eat."

"How can I say, no? I have nothing planned for New Year's Day and I haven't had enough champagne to develop a hangover."

"Oh good! Thank you so much, Jax. You're a good man. Come on up here at 9:30 and we'll ride together."

"I'll be here. Good night, Grace."

Chapter 20

Brooke sat at the small desk in her hotel room hunched over the blueprints for the Java Hut and the surrounding buildings. She startled when the door flew open and crashed against the doorstop. Her roommate and subordinate on the Secret Service detail, Tatianna Sweeney, burst into the room.

"This weather sucks." Anna stomped into the kitchenette and poured a large mug of coffee. "How do people survive the wind and the cold?"

Brooke laughed. "Well… They probably don't wear leggings and a T-shirt to run outside in January. You do know there's a gym here in the hotel and it's heated."

"Very funny. The two decrepit treadmills in the so-called gym were taken by two old men walking at like a mile an hour. I had no choice but to brave the cold if I wanted to get my workout in today. I'll jump in a nice hot shower and then we can go over the security plan one more time."

She nodded agreement, pleased that Anna shared her commitment to detail.

The two women had met at Brooke's Secret Service orientation. Gary Stewart was thrilled to have Brooke on board and had introduced her to his newest recruit, Anna. They had a lot in common, had hit it off immediately and had trained together. All five foot seven inches of Anna was solid muscle. She easily kept up with the men in the

Agency and had spurred Brooke to train harder until Brooke could beat Anna and everyone else on the team in a race. She had transformed her body into solid muscle with Anna as her workout partner.

Brooke had recommended Anna to Gary for inclusion on the elite protection team for the Vice President that Brooke headed. As she had expected, Anna worked efficiently with her, and a friendship was born.

Anna emerged out of the bedroom dressed, similar to Brooke, in a charcoal gray pantsuit and starched, white button-down shirt. Her wet hair was pulled back in a tight bun. She tossed Brooke a protein bar and perched on the arm of the couch near the desk.

"So what's the schedule for Panda and Hottie?" Anna said.

The Secret Service used code names for Vice Presidents and sometimes their family members. Agnew was Pathfinder, Quale was Scorecard, and Pence was Hoosier. Grace Burrows was given the code name Panda because the San Diego Zoo had named a panda Grace after her.

"Who's Hottie?" Brooke said.

"Grace is bringing a guest with her."

"I know she is, but I didn't know we gave him a code name."

"Not officially. But when you see him you'll understand why I came up with one for him. You missed seeing him at the party where I worked the perimeter with Brad last week when you were still in Washington meeting with Gary. All I'll say is that I would let that man flip my pancakes anytime."

Anna smirked when Brooke burst out laughing.

They focused on the diagrams and had everything buttoned down when Brooke sent out a group text.

—Rolling in ten.—

Exactly nine minutes later Brooke joined the rest of her team in front of the hotel. She hopped into the first sleek black Suburban idling at the curb.

Brooke was proud of the team she had assembled. The three men sitting in the backseat were retired Green Berets, assigned as snipers. They would station on the rooftops surrounding the coffee shop.

Anna rode in the counter assault team truck with the rest of the personal protection team bound for the condo building where Grace lived. During the ride, Brooke went over the security plan in her mind making sure she hadn't missed anything that might compromise the safety of the Vice President Elect. She was confident that her team was prepared.

The car parked in front of the Java Hut, discharged Brooke and the sniper team and pulled away from the curb. Brooke inserted her coms earpiece and waited on the sidewalk. Adrenaline surged through her making her impervious to the cold. The shop front reminded Brooke of Pops' Café. She had a flashback to the first time she had seen Jax in front of the cafe. The memory still took her breath away.

She didn't have long to dwell on the past. The motorcade arrived launching her into action. Brooke strode to the truck, her gaze constantly scanning the vicinity as Anna and the rest of the protection detail created a human shield at the side of the car where the protectees would emerge. Car doors slammed as the vetted members of the Press readied to cover the event.

Brooke pulled on the backdoor handle of the

armored limo and swung open the rear door expecting Grace to exit. Instead Jax Rosso jumped out of the car, reached back inside, clasped Grace's hand and helped her step out of the car. Brooke's jaw dropped. She stood rooted to the spot still clinging to the door handle.

Jax turned and caught sight of Brooke. He jolted slightly, his smile disappeared, and his lips pursed in a straight line.

"Good morning, Brooke." Grace's soft voice broke through her shock. "I want you to meet my friend, Jax."

He didn't say a word.

Grace gazed up at Jax. "Brooke is the agent in charge of my security detail."

"Nice to meet you," he muttered.

Jax put his arm around Grace's shoulders and led her into the coffee shop surrounded by Anna and the team. Brooke slammed the door shut with more force than necessary and then brought up the rear of the detail.

Applause erupted as Grace made her entrance. Brooke took her post inside in front of the door. Anna and the rest of the team formed a security circle on the perimeter. Their eyes constantly darted around the shop. The tables were pushed together to form one large table in the center of the room. Grace and Jax took the two empty seats at the head of the table.

A waitress approached Grace to take her breakfast order. Her hand holding an order pad shook. "What would you like ma'am?" Her voice cracked, surely with nerves.

Grace smiled at the young woman. "I would love a mug of tea with lemon, please."

"And you sir?"

"I'll have a venti salted caramel mocha Frappuccino

with four pumps of caramel, three pumps of mocha and extra whipped cream."

The waitress knit her brow and wrote like mad on her order pad keeping her head bent. Conversations around the table stopped as if the group collectively thought, Who the heck *is* this guy?

Jax burst out laughing. "I'm teasing. A mug of black coffee would be perfect."

"That was very believable pretention, Jax." Grace chuckled.

He huffed a laugh. "My ex dictated that order to me every day. The barista at our local coffee shop knew me by name. I think she felt sorry for me."

Brooke overheard the conversation. *My ex* were the only words that registered. He had obviously moved on from her to Grace. The thought opened old wounds and searing jealousy shot through her. She narrowed her eyes against the pain. And then she squared her shoulders and focused on the job refusing distraction by him or anyone else.

Grace thanked her supporters and repeated her promise to work tirelessly to represent them in Washington at President Matthew Campbell's side. She fielded questions around the table and encouraged her constituents to voice their concerns and wish list for the new administration.

Each minute of the hour they spent at the coffee shop was painful for Brooke. No matter how she tried to ignore Jax, his voice was like a siren's song calling to her. The people sitting with him at the table seemed charmed and made him just as much a center of attention as Grace. He never took his focus off Grace. Brooke didn't feel his attention drift to her once.

Grace caught Brooke's eye with a slight nod.

Brooke tapped her earpiece to transmit. "Panda on the move in five."

She walked to a position behind Grace's chair. "Madam Vice President, we have to leave now so you can get to your next appointment."

Grace stood up, thanked everyone again and followed Brooke to the door. Anna stepped through the doorway first. Brooke waited in front of Grace and Jax until Anna signaled the "all clear" and she could lead the couple out to the car. Brooke closed the rear door of the limo and breathed a sigh of relief when the motorcade sped away.

The sniper team joined Brooke at the curb, and they piled into the waiting black SUV.

Outside the hotel, Brooke thanked her team. "Great job everyone. We leave for Midway this afternoon, so grab something to eat and meet back here at 1700 hours."

Inside the suite, Brooke headed straight to her bedroom tugging off her suit jacket as she advanced to the closet. She shed her pants and blouse, hung them on hangers to put on later for the flight to D.C., and then dressed in insulated running clothes determined to pound any thoughts of Jax out of her system.

"The guys said they would grab a couple of pizzas in two hours if we want to join them." Anna leaned against the bedroom door.

"That sounds great." She dug in her purse for her wallet and then handed Anna money. "My treat. I'll be back in an hour."

Brooke stuck air buds in her ears, pulled on a knit headband, donned wraparound sunglasses and pocketed her phone.

"Damn you look like a ninja." Anna laughed.

Brooke looked down at her midnight black outfit: high rise leggings, a fleece shirt, and insulated vest. "Perfect. That's the look I was going for."

She paced along the sidewalk in the direction of Lake Michigan for a few minutes to stretch out her muscles. The wind had died down and the sun offered some warmth. Tension eased, readying for her workout. Seeing Jax again was hard enough but seeing him with someone else was crippling, even though Brooke wholeheartedly admired that someone else. His coldness was far more frost biting than the weather.

She jogged a couple blocks and then accelerated into a run towards Navy Pier. The looming Centennial Wheel with its climate-controlled gondolas turned slowly. More people milled around the Pier than Brooke expected considering it was New Year's Day. If she weren't working, she'd start the new year in front of a fire with a good book rather than freezing in a city she had never visited before, ruing the day she had met Jaxson Rosso.

Brooke ran down the sidewalk bordering the lakefront and stopped for a minute to observe the crazies doing the New Year's polar plunge in the freezing water. Brrr. It made her colder just watching them.

Footfalls sounded behind her, and she ran faster. She stopped at a red light and jogged in place waiting for the green pedestrian sign to illuminate.

"Don't hurt Grace," came a deep voice from behind her.

She would know that voice anywhere. Brooke turned, fisted her hands against her hips and glared at Jax.

****

The last person that Jax wanted to encounter again that day was Brooke, but she had followed his jogging route, and the red light had all but crashed him into her. One more block and he would have turned around and escaped without saying a word to her.

Did he really want to escape? The scent of honeysuckle ignited his senses and brought home how much he still missed her.

"What did you say?" she spat out.

"I said don't hurt Grace."

Dressed all in black she looked fierce and very sexy. Against all reason he still wanted her.

"What a stupid thing to say to me," she barked. He opened his mouth to deliver a retort, but she cut him off. "I took an oath to protect and serve the Vice President with my life. I don't take that oath lightly no matter who she chooses to squire her around."

"Your track record precedes you, *Agent* Pellington. You're an expert at hurting people."

"Wipe that smug look off your face, you big ass." She held up her hand. "I'll do everything in my power to make sure *no one* hurts your girlfriend because it's my job."

"Was it your *job* to sleep with me?" He almost regretted uttering those words a split second later. The crushed expression on Brooke's face brought a pinch of guilt.

She remained silent for a few beats. Then she slowly removed her sunglasses, narrowed her eyes and unleashed her fury. "Really? That's your question after months of... no communication between us? I did my job. I helped to put a traitor in jail. I saved your ass and cleared you. Whether you believe it or not, I cleared your mother, too, in the process. Stop acting like a victim. I didn't force you into the bedroom that night."

Brooke sucked in a breath and brushed a tear off her cheek.

He reached out to touch her, but she ducked away from his reach. Her eyes met his.

"I am so sorry for the loss of your mom. In a very short time, I loved Sofia."

"Brooke—"

"Let me finish. I loved *you*, Jax. Stupid me, I thought you were falling in love with me, too. I thought we had a future together after the case was over and I could explain everything. But you never gave me the chance. You need to stop blaming me and start blaming the person who is really responsible for your mother's death. Thurston Baxter ruined your mother's life. Not me."

She turned her back on him and sped away towards Navy Pier. Rather than follow her, he stood watching her retreat until she disappeared from view while her passionate words rang in his mind. Brooke was right. He had blamed her for Sofia's death, and he should have blamed Baxter.

Brooke said she loved him. That much rang true even though she *had* deceived him. He had never stopped loving her despite his grief and confusion. Since she had used the past tense, he wasn't sure how she now felt about him.

Jax made up his mind. He would win Brooke back somehow.

Chapter 21

Jax began his planning to recapture Brooke's heart right after his encounter with her during his morning run. Inside his condo, he tossed the keys in a dish on a console table in the foyer, tuned the TV to a football game, and sat down in front of his laptop. Since seeing her at the Grand Jury hearing and Sofia's subsequent death after Baxter was indicted, Jax had refused to find Brooke Pellington online or investigate her further except to skim the article reporting her and Michael Lynch's pivotal roles in gathering evidence and coordinating the arrests.

He gave multiple AI commands and sat back absorbing any personal information about Brooke he could glean from the web. It wasn't much. Understandably there was a large body of information about her father since he had undergone Congressional scrutiny before he was named FBI Director two administrations ago. By all accounts he would retain the office when Matthew Campbell became president in a few weeks.

His wife, Brooke's mom, died of cancer when Brooke was a toddler. Her maiden name was James. One piece of Brooke's deception fell into place. Brooke was a high school track star and National Honor Student recruited to Indiana University where she received her undergrad—Summa Cum Laude. Graduation photos of

Brooke's FBI Quantico class revealed a few more details. Her story about her lifelong friend Kay possibly wasn't too far from the truth. She and Kay were depicted at the graduation with their arms around each other beaming at the camera. AI identified them both. Mike apparently was an instructor at Quantico which might explain how he met his fiancée.

He studied Brooke's face in the photo with Kay. She was lovely, stunning, take your breath away Brooke James through and through. Sweetness and softness were written in her smile, just as he remembered her.

Another photo depicted her with Gary Stewart, identified as an instructor like Mike, now apparently Brooke's superior at the Secret Service. No photos of Brooke with her father at all. That gave him pause.

Jax spent a few more minutes tapping on his keyboard. Except for a couple blurry photos of Brooke in the background where Grace Burrows was front and center, he couldn't find current mentions of Brooke online.

Between that day and the Inauguration, he talked with Grace on the phone almost every evening. She was lonely and admittedly so was he. They found fast friends in each other, and he was glad and excited to be her escort at such a storied occasion as the upcoming Inauguration. Plus, he'd see Brooke again when he was determined to make amends. He'd occasionally insinuate questions about her Secret Service detail to Grace in the hopes that he'd learn more about Brooke. Grace practically idealized Brooke describing her as a badass, a sharpshooter, meticulous, devoted, discreet and above all, brave. The fresh information didn't jibe with his impressions of Brooke James…except for her handling of some of the rowdier men she had come into contact with when they were together.

Together. Jax wanted that again.

****

Brooke didn't spearhead the security team that accompanied Grace's motorcade to O'Hare on January eighteenth for the trip to Washington, but she was standing on the tarmac where the government plane taxied and then discharged Grace and Jax to ride in yet another motorcade to Blair House. Brooke was all business, and he couldn't capture her attention with his smile. He wouldn't try to force any connection in that setting and wondered when he might get the chance as he slipped into the seat next to Grace and was whisked to Blair House.

Jax unpacked in a guest bedroom room with a four poster, canopied bed in the historic residence across the street from the White House that had housed Vice Presidents Elect and visiting dignitaries. Grace had told him that he would be left to his own devices the couple days leading up to the Inauguration when she would move to the Vice-Presidential residence at the Naval Observatory. She told Jax that he was welcome to stay there the night of the Inauguration and for as long as he wanted to visit D.C.

He hadn't made up his mind about a return date to Chicago, hopeful that Brooke would let him back into her life. Jax had asked Dryden if he could be open-ended about vacation time. Dryden hadn't hesitated to approve. His matchmaker boss and friend heartily endorsed Jax's relationship with Grace, even insinuating that he might become the Second Gentleman soon.

That wasn't a remote possibility. Not just because of

his feelings for Brooke but also because of Grace's feelings for Jax: one hundred percent friendship zone. She had confided in Jax that she doubted she'd ever remarry or even fall in love again. Of course, that could change if she met the right man. He was not that guy.

Jax had visited Washington before when he was a kid. Sofia had saved for years to take him to the country's Capitol. He would enjoy wandering around the Mall and visiting the Lincoln, Jefferson and War Memorials again in her memory. He'd love to have Brooke on his arm to explore with him. But it was obvious that she couldn't spare a moment engaged in her duties to protect Grace during a time of massive public exposure.

Jax's massive public exposure began, too, when Inauguration Day dawned. Dressed in a black suit, white dress shirt and dark navy-blue tie, he met Grace at the portico of the residence and the whirlwind began.

****

Brooke hadn't slept well the night before January twentieth. She was itchy to put her, please God, perfect security plan in motion having assessed all current threats. There were plenty. Although Campbell's victory was decisive, there was polarity along party lines and opposition fanatics in the general population. Most disturbing were Intel reports of the threat of foreign terrorists. Campbell and Burrows were seen as strong and unyielding with the global agenda that got them elected. Death threats were common.

She and Anna bookended the Veep during the swearing in at the East Portico of the Capitol Building. Grace apparently had asked Jax to hold the Bible upon which she rested her hand and recited her oath of office after the Supreme Court Justice. Brooke swallowed the surge of bitter jealously that clogged her throat standing at her post watching Jax partner with Grace. Her fondness for and devotion to Grace couldn't be compromised by a man. Period. She sucked it up. She would deal despite her broken heart. Like she always did.

Vice President Burrows and her "Hottie" escort processed from the East to the West portico of the Capitol to attend the Presidential Inauguration between a phalanx of Brooke and her Secret Service detail. Once her protectees were seated in the gallery behind bullet proof shields, Brooke relaxed some standing strategically with her team outside for the ceremony. It was a mild, sunny day. Although the major players in the event would still need coats and overcoats to wear along the parade route down Pennsylvania Avenue to the White House. They had chosen to walk.

But first came hours of high alert for Brooke during the pomp and ceremony of the day: the oath of office while First Lady Kimberly Campell and their three children held the Bible for the president; the presidential address, poetry, song, blessings and bands. The luncheon hosted by Congress in the Capitol Building following the ceremony outside was more secure, but Brooke still didn't relax for a second.

Camera crews and Press were everywhere. Vetting was immaculate for journalist attendees but that didn't stop Brooke from constantly scanning the room for threats. It was necessary for her to shadow Grace closely which meant she remained near Jax—literally too close for comfort. She bristled when a reporter thrust a microphone in Jax's face and insinuated that perhaps Grace Burrows wouldn't remain a widow.

His response encouraged hope in Brooke and then

squashed any hope that she might have a future with him.

"I'm honored to escort the Vice President today. Grace and I are close friends. She is still dealing with the loss of her husband, and I've lost someone dear to me, too."

His mourning Sofia would always come between them.

Cheering and crowd noise along the parade route had Brooke intensely concentrating on her team's communications through her earpiece while she surveyed the area wishing she had eyes behind her head. When they arrived at the White House and Brooke ushered Panda and Hottie into their limo in the motorcade bound for the Vice-Presidential residence, Brooke had some respite from constant tension.

Grace intended to take a nap before the evening's demands and Jax apparently followed suit. Brooke couldn't concern herself with his whereabouts. Tonight's trotting from ball to ball would challenge her team more than ever. She should rest, too. But that was impossible.

****

The sight of Jax in a tuxedo robbed Brooke's breath. Grace looked amazing in her sapphire blue, satin gown and Brooke was jealous not only of her escort but also of her ability to wear the uncomplicated dress. She wished she could wow Jax with her formal wear, but the jacketed black evening suit, although stylish, wasn't enough wow factor owing to functionality. Brooke needed to conceal her weapon, and the suit worked. At least the camisole beneath her jacket was a bit low cut and evening sexy. She thought she caught Jax's gaze linger on her. But that was probably her wishful thinking.

Despite her need for vigilance, Brooke enjoyed her

involvement in the evening's festivities. Matthew Campbell and Kimberly Campbell presented a gorgeous, classy couple to the world. They were the youngest presidential couple in history and Grace held that distinction, too, as Vice President. The four honorees glowed in front of the crowds and made Brooke yearn to be enfolded in Jax's arms, as Grace was, for each dance at the Commander In Chief Ball and the Liberty Ball. Grace looked like she belonged there with Jax. He fit the role of a political spouse perfectly and she marveled at his smooth dancing style. She thought she knew everything about Jaxson Rosso from the case file. Apparently not.

The Starlight Ball was the last of the evening. By that time Brooke was exhausted and done with the sameness of the events and the constant stress of protecting Grace while suppressing personal jealousy. Regardless, she stood ramrod erect stage left while the foursome stood center stage accepting thunderous applause from the candidates' donors. In the din, Brooke detected static in her earpiece. She pressed on it and heard distinct sharp cracks coming from outside the ballroom doors.

"Brad report. What was that?"

No answer from him. There could only be one explanation.

"Shooter," she said into her mic.

And then Brooke didn't hesitate for a split second. She rushed toward Grace and dove just as she heard the ballroom doors burst open, and a barrage of rapid fire had the crowd screaming. She soft tackled Grace and covered her body with her own as flying bullets whizzed past her.

She heard Jax yell, "Brooke!" and then felt his weight on top of her just as a searing pain lanced her side and the world went gray and fuzzy. She perceived three shooters wearing balaclavas spraying bullets at the stage.

From her prone position, still shielding Grace, Brooke reached for her gun. She aimed, her hand steady despite her wound and the insane amount of adrenaline coursing through her. She hit one shooter squarely in the heart, and he folded into a heap on the floor. The other two were dropped one by one by her team.

"Clear," came a shout.

Brooke tried to rise but all she could do was roll off Grace onto her back. Jax was a dead weight that rolled with her. Sirens blared and Jax was hefted onto a stretcher.

She pressed her hand to her side which came back sticky with blood. Just as her vision dimmed she witnessed Grace, Matthew and Kimberly rushed off the stage by Anna and the president's security team.

"Good," she said.

The world went black.

Chapter 22

Two ambulances, a caravan of police vehicles with lights flashing, and the Secret Service sleek black SUVs raced the nine miles to Walter Reed Hospital unimpeded by traffic. Military personnel had cleared the route.

Jax regained consciousness in one of the speeding ambulances. Sirens keened as if drilling into his brain. He whipped his head back dislodging the oxygen mask from over his mouth.

"Brooke," he whispered.

"You're okay. We'll be at the hospital soon." The female paramedic reattached his mask with one hand. She pressed one hand heavily against his shoulder.

"Brooke," Jax said beneath the oxygen mask.

The paramedic arched over him. "What did you say, Mr. Rosso?"

As if someone dimmed the lights before switching them off, Jax's vision moved from gray to black.

****

He felt like he was floating. *Where am I? What happened?*

Jax thought he recognized a woman's muffled voice but couldn't identify who spoke.

"I already lost an agent today. I can't lose anyone else," she said.

Grace. She lost an agent. He struggled to open his eyes against the strong opposing desire to stay in that peaceful, floaty state.

Jax wrenched his eyes open and blinked repeatedly to bring Grace into focus. She sat at the side of his bed with her cell phone pressed to her ear. He stirred in the bed causing the soft beeping next to his ear to shriek.

"He's awake, I have to go." Grace sprang out of the chair and clasped his hand. "It's okay Jax. You're safe."

"I heard you say you lost…" He could barely frame the question. "Did Brooke die?"

"No, no. Brooke just got out of surgery. The doctors are optimistic that she'll be fine."

"Who then?"

"We lost Brad." Tears streamed down Grace's face. "I'm very sorry."

Sleep dragged him down.

****

When Jax awoke, Grace still clasped his hand from her bedside seat haloed by sunrise rosy light filtering through the plate glass windows in the room.

"You're still here," he croaked.

"Where else would I be?" She smiled and squeezed his hand.

Jax pushed himself up into a sitting position, threw off the bedsheet and swung his legs over the side of the bed. Alarms blared from the machines attached to his body.

"Whoa Jax, what are you doing? You have to lie back down. I'll get your doctor."

"I have to see Brooke."

"Oh Jax. Are you sure that's a good idea? From what you told me when you saw her in Chicago she was pretty upset with you. And she has a right to be."

"I know. I *have* to tell her that I don't blame her for

Mom's death. I love her, Grace."

Grace blew out a breath. "Well I don't want to stand in the way of that…I promise I'll do everything I can to help you. But first, the doctor has to check you out."

She pushed the call button. As if his medical team stood vigilant right outside the door, they responded within seconds, surrounded his bed, took vitals, checked readings and changed the dressing on his wound. His doctor explained that they had cleanly removed a bullet from his shoulder and there were no complications. Jax had lost a lot of blood and needed total bedrest for the next few days.

The medical team left the room. Jax threw the sheet off again and sat up with effort. "Now I'll go see Brooke."

"You heard the doctor, Jax. He said you needed bedrest for the next few days. Please lie down."

"I won't be able to rest at all until I see Brooke with my own eyes. Grace, with or without your help, I'm going to see Brooke now." Jax swung his legs over the side of the bed and stood for moment. He closed his eyes and grabbed the edge of the bed as he swayed.

"Sit back down now you stubborn man. Let me get some help." She marched to the door and pulled it open.

"Jeremy can you please get a wheelchair transport for Mr. Rosso?" Her tone made it clear that she expected immediate action.

"Yes ma'am," came the reply.

"Who's Jeremy?" Jax slipped his good arm into the robe that Grace held open for him.

She draped the robe over his right shoulder. "One of Brooke's subordinates on my Secret Service detail."

The wheelchair transport arrived in minutes. Jax

leaned heavily on the male attendant to get into the chair. He sat breathing deeply while his IV bag was hung from the pole on the back of the chair.

Grace watched him hawk-eyed. "Are you sure you're up for this? You literally are as white as those sheets."

"I'm positive. I promise I'll follow all the doctor's orders *after* I see Brooke."

"I'm holding you to that."

Grace walked alongside his wheelchair down the deserted hallway. They turned a corner and reached a small sitting area in front of a room where two uniformed cops stood guard. The attendant pushed the wheelchair to the door and made to open it.

"Halt!" A tall, unsmiling man jumped up from the sofa and blocked the door. It only took Jax a few seconds to recognize the FBI Director.

"Where do you think you're going?" He stared Jax down. "I don't want you anywhere near my daughter."

Director Pellington crossed his arms over his chest and speared Grace with his steely gaze. "This man is the reason my daughter is no longer one of the best FBI agents I have ever had under my command."

"Stand down, Director." Grace closed the distance between her and Pellington. "That's an order." She stood unyielding, a tiny steel rod scowling up at him.

"You have no right—"

"Sir, as Vice President, I have every right," she interjected. "Have you had a chance to review the video of the assassination attempt?"

He wagged his head.

"I suggest you watch the video. Your daughter threw herself in front of the bullet meant for me and Mr. Rosso threw himself on top of your daughter to protect her. He took a bullet meant for her. If Mr. Rosso didn't block that bullet, according to forensics, it would have hit your daughter in the head. All Mr. Rosso wants is a few minutes to check on Brooke. It's within my power to make that happen for him, so sit your ass down." Her words left Brooke's father speechless.

Grace nodded to one of the policemen guarding Brooke's room. He opened the door.

Jax was wheeled into the room followed by the vice president not daring to look at Pellington's face as he passed by him. The attendant positioned him at the side of the bed, locked the wheels and left the room.

"If you feel worse or need anything at all, push the call button or just holler." Grace glanced tenderly at Brooke and then left the room.

Alone with her, Jax took Brooke's soft, limp hand in his. The sight of her pale, waxen face terrified him. Tubes and wires attached to the massive amount of machinery that encircled her bed snaked from seemingly all parts of her body. He sat quietly for a few minutes and watched her chest rise and fall, weak with gratitude that she was still breathing.

Thank you, Lord.

"Hi," he whispered.

Jax didn't expect her to respond but found himself wishing with all his heart that she would. Maybe a blink. He squeezed her hand gently, but she didn't squeeze his hand back. Still, the doctors were optimistic. Jax had to believe her strength would carry her through.

"I'm sorry for being such a jackass, Brooke. I was wrong. The last time I saw you, you said I was blaming the wrong person for what happened to Mom. You're

197

right. I wanted to tell you that sooner but at the very least I had planned to tell you this after the Inauguration."

He brought her hand to his lips and kissed it. "I know you think Grace and I are a couple, and I'm sorry that I let you believe that. We aren't and never have been. She's become a very good friend who, come to think of it, reminds me of you—fierce and protective. I wish you could have seen her school your father a few minutes ago. He tried to bar me from coming into your room. She made it happen. Believe it or not she actually told him to sit his ass down. Even more unbelievable; he did.

"Bet no one has spoken to him like that in a long time." Jax paused. "Or maybe ever."

He grinned at the memory. "I don't want to leave you, Brooke. I want to stay in here with you and protect you and make sure you're safe.

"And when you're recovered, I want to spend my life with you." Those words flowed easily. Jax realized that he meant what he said. He wanted to marry Brooke.

"Did I ever tell you how Hunter proposed to Lyndsey? He showed up one day at her door with two wiggly puppies aka Mabel and Millie. He had had their collars engraved. Mabel's read, Will you? And Millie's followed with, Marry me? When Lyndsey took the little ones in her arms Hunter got down on one knee, held out a ring box and officially proposed. I guess Hunter had a lot to live up to.

"His mom had worked in a pub when she was in college. Peggy loved the job so much that even though she graduated as a certified teacher she decided to keep her fulltime bartender job. Hunter's dad, Paul met Peggy at the pub and was smitten with her at first sight.

"They dated around her work schedule until the

owners of the pub decided to retire and put the property up for sale. The land was in a prime location and developers were interested in building condos on the site. Peggy was heartbroken.

"Paul came in one night for a late dinner before the bar had shut down for good. As usual, he waited for Peggy to close up so he could take her home. While she finished cleaning in the kitchen Paul lit candles and placed them all over the bar. When she came into the barroom ready to leave, he was on one knee with a jewelry box in his palm.

"She accepted his proposal and eagerly opened the box. A set of keys was tucked inside.

"Paul had bought the bar for her. Peggy's Place was born that night. She was ecstatic. But she also teased him about the lack of a ring. He supplied it the very next day.

"Have you ever thought about a marriage proposal? Until recently I never gave it much thought—"

The door swished open, and a nurse poked her head inside the room. "I'm sorry. You need to leave so you both can rest. I've ordered transport back to your room. I'll be back in a few minutes to tend to her."

With effort, Jax stood, planted his hands carefully on either side of Brooke's body, leaned over, kissed her forehead and started to sit back down in the wheelchair.

"Red Silverado," came a breathy whisper.

Shocked, he hung over her, staring at her face. But he detected no change in Brooke. Jax sat down heavily in the chair. The attendant hurried inside the room, bent to unlock the chair's wheels and then pushed Jax toward the door.

"And a ring."

The transport attendant stopped short.

"You heard that?" Jax turned his head toward Brooke's bed.

"I thought I heard something." The attendant stared at Brooke, too.

She didn't show any sign of consciousness, but Jax smiled anyway having the attendant as a witness.

He sagged in his seat suddenly exhausted to the bone. Jax made a snap decision once outside of her room in the sitting area. "Can you please wheel me over in front of that gentleman?" He pointed at Pellington.

"I have nothing to say to you," the director barked.

"That's okay. I don't need you to say anything. I just wanted to let you know that I'm in love with your daughter."

Brooke's father scowled at Jax, straight lipped. His cold slate gray eyes bore into him.

Jax could imagine a parade of subordinates withering under Director Pellington's icy glare. But the man didn't intimidate him at all.

"The past hours have proven the old cliché: Life is short. I don't plan on wasting a minute from now on. I'm going to ask your daughter to marry me. I would appreciate your permission, but I'll propose to her as soon as she's well whether you give me your blessing or not."

Jax's request met with silence. The two men locked gazes. Neither one was willing to blink first.

He was about to give up and go back to his room when Brooke's father piped up, "I was told that I have you to thank for saving my daughter's life. Thank you. I give you my permission to ask my daughter to marry you. And I'll be very happy when she turns you down as I believe she will."

"I'm ready to leave now," Jax told the transport attendant.

Grace waited for him in his room. "Oh Jax. You look like hell. Let me get someone to help you into bed."

The pain in his shoulder was excruciating. He was grateful once he was settled back in bed and his nurse had administered some IV pain medicine. Grace left Jax to sleep after he assured her that he would follow all medical direction and not go wandering around the hospital searching for Brooke again.

The door closed softly behind the Vice President of the United States.

Before he gave in to sleep, he placed a call. "Dryden, I need your help."

Chapter 23

Disorientation persisted for Brooke during her hospitalization. Time slipped away from her. The only way she could keep track of the passage of days was through repetitive hospital routine. Vitals every four hours, wee hour of the morning blood draws that yanked you out of fitful sleep, dressing changes, respiratory therapy and daily ill-fated attempts at walking under her own steam. She had yet to make it outside of her room.

The blessed every few hours doses of pain meds helped. The side of her torso where the bullet had entered and her insides where it had wreaked havoc speared her with constant pain. She both dreaded and looked forward to the excruciating rehab she'd undergo before she could resume her duties. Grace had assured her that she wouldn't accept a replacement to head her security detail—only a temporary substitute. Brooke couldn't wait to put recuperation behind her and get back to work.

Grace was a daily visitor—unbelievable to Brooke since the Veep had taken up her myriad of duties post Inauguration and the president's agenda was aggressive. But she wouldn't hear of staying away no matter how many times Brooke assured her that she was fine and was in the best of hands. Where Grace went, so went her detail, so Brooke received short visits from Anna and Jeremy and the guys. The problem there was that they made her laugh and that hurt like hell. She asked Grace about Jax only once not wanting to pry into her protectee's personal life no matter how tempting. Grace had assured her that Jax was on the mend and comfortable in the Vice President's residence.

Brooke was swimmy-headed most of her waking hours and drifted to sleep after minor exertion. Occasionally, she thought that she had heard her father's voice amid the cacophony of unrecognizable voices that surrounded her when her eyes were closed. And that made no sense to her at all.

She enjoyed clarity only in her vivid dreams. Brooke had dreamed that Jax apologized to her and loved her. He had told her romantic stories and had alluded to giving her a romantic story of her own. How she wished that were true in her real world.

Brooke had hounded Grace to pull strings to release her from Walter Reed. Bless her generous, grateful heart, Grace had planned in detail for Brooke's continued medical care at home, the nurse had drawn a smiley face on the treatment grease board and discharge day arrived. After she had dressed, she sagged, winded and exhausted on the edge of her bed. Anna had brought her FBI sweats to wear so that she wouldn't have to dress in the bloody evening outfit that she had on when brought to the hospital. But wearing those clothes would be preferable. Because the FBI insignia reminded her that she had lost Jax and could only be happy in her dreams.

The door opened bringing with it a waft of hospital smell and citrusy aftershave. Gary approached her bed grinning broadly.

"You're looking pretty fit considering." He flopped into the vinyl covered lazy boy chair bedside her bed. He gave a sweeping wave of his hand in her direction. "Are you trying to tell me something?"

"What do you mean?"

"FBI. Are you deserting me to work for your father again?"

She broke into a laugh and then stopped short at the twist of pain in her gut. "Quit making me laugh. It hurts too much."

"Sorry." He gazed at her intently. "You still haven't answered my question."

"I can't believe you're asking. No, I'm not deserting you. I don't regret my decision one bit. And I never will."

"Not even after what happened?"

"Especially after what happened. I'm dedicated to Grace. And any other official I have the honor of protecting. I only wish I were ready to go back to work right now."

Gary closed his eyes and wagged his head. "You're something, Pellington. I'm beyond proud."

"And well you should be," came her dad's unmistakable deep voice from the open doorway.

"Dad…I mean, sir. I didn't know you were here…"

"He's been outside your door 24/7 since your admission." Gary rose from his chair.

Brooke gaped at her father. "You *have?*"

"Where else would I be?" he snapped. "Good." Pellington scowled at the transport attendant who appeared behind him. "Help her into the chair."

"Take care, Brooke. I'll be in touch." Gary breezed out the door.

The attendant rushed to her bedside. Brooke stood slowly, leaned on his arm and sat down in the wheelchair.

"Thank you." She hoped her soft voice would gloss

over her father's barking at people. Would her dad never stop treating everyone like his underlings? Including her?

Dad inched the attendant aside and pushed the wheelchair forward confusing Brooke. She had assumed that Gary was there to take her home. Her father wanted to ignore his position and take the time to drive her to Virginia? Was she dreaming?

No. Because if she were, Jax would be wheeling her through hospital corridors, not her distant father.

Outside in the main building's parking garage, the director's armored SUV idled ahead. His driver rushed towards them and covered Brooke with a warm lap blanket. She felt giddy as if making a prison break and finally breathing in fresh air. That the air was January cold didn't bother her a bit.

Her father set her in motion again. But instead of wheeling her to the SUV's door, he rolled her down a slight ramp in front of his car into the garage. Dead ahead Jax leaned against the rear bumper of a Silverado truck. His left arm was in a sling.

Brooke's jaw dropped. Their gazes met and locked. He dropped to one knee and held out a velvet ring box in her direction.

"What the heck?" she whispered.

Dad pushed her closer to Jax's position on the garage floor, moved in front of the chair to lock the wheels and then stood in front of her. "The silly man. I should never have given him my permission."

Her eyes widened to saucers. "Permission to what?"

"To ask you to marry him."

"He…you… *what*?"

"I'll be in the car waiting for you to send him

running." He walked away and left her gaping at Jax in front of the gleaming truck. What she had taken as a dream wasn't a dream at all. *Have you ever thought about a marriage proposal?*

Oh my gosh.

"Hi," Jax said.

She narrowed her eyes. "You said you were a jackass, and you were wrong."

"I am and I was."

Brooke nodded her head. "You said you wanted to spend your life with me."

"Mm hm. That's why I'm in this, by the way, *very* uncomfortable position right now."

"So this is a proposal? And you asked my father for my…hand?"

"I did. And he said yes. Only because one, he thanked me for saving his daughter's life and—"

"You saved my life? Nobody told me that."

"Well, I guess I dove over your body and the bullet that might have hit you, hit me instead."

"Wow, Jax. I don't know what to say…"

"No need. I'd do it again in a heartbeat. The other reason your father said yes was that he didn't think for a minute that you'd accept a marriage proposal from me."

Brooke threw back her head and laughed. Her delight overshadowed the pain that laughing caused her. "My father's right about a lot of things. But not necessarily this."

The smile he beamed at her ignited months of repressed desire. His handsome face…his gorgeous body…his sweetness and honesty and strength had haunted her through the separation that she had caused and what had seemed the permanent separation that he had caused when the investigation had come to a head.

All she had wanted since she left him in Luna Beach as Brooke James was for him to understand and throw his arms around Brooke Pellington.

"So what do you have there?" She pointed to the ring box.

"You have to accept my proposal before you see."

She bit back a smile and waved her hand in front of her. "Well get on with it, then."

"I don't want to live without you, Brooke. Not ever again. I love you with all that I am. Will you marry me?"

The last thing she had expected that day had materialized. She didn't know how to contain her glee. Happiness bubbled out of her at her reply, "Yes, Jax. I love you with all my heart."

He got to his feet with a slight grimace and approached her wheelchair grinning madly. He handed her the ring box, and she whipped it open. Inside she found a Chevrolet key fob.

Brooke picked up the key and pushed a button on the fob. The locks of the truck in front of her disengaged with audible clicks.

"Red Silverado," she said.

"You like it?"

"I love it, Jax. It's my dream car."

"Color okay? They call it Victory Red."

She grinned at him. "Couldn't be more perfect."

"Ready to try her out? Of course, I'll drive for now."

"Sure." Brooke eyed the car. "I'm not sure that I can climb in there."

"That's not a problem." He rushed to the side of the truck and opened the passenger door.

And then he returned to stand in front of her leaning

forward. "Put your arms around my neck."

Brooke hesitated. "How in the world will you carry me with one arm?"

He straightened and slipped his arm out of the sling. "I won't put too much weight on the wounded arm. Don't worry."

Jax leaned toward her again.

"One second. Can you take me over to my father first?"

"Sure."

He disengaged the wheel locks and rolled her onto the sidewalk alongside the director's car. The rear window slid down just like in a spy flick and she gazed into her father's eyes. "Daddy, I've accepted Jax's proposal."

She thought she detected a slight upturn of his lips. Was the formidable director smiling? "You haven't called me Daddy in years."

"I know. You're not my boss anymore. I thought it was time."

"I'm proud of you, Brooke. "

Her father had never told her that in her memory even though she had endlessly sought to hear those words for him since she was a little kid. "Thank you. I'm very proud of you, too."

"But I've never received the Congressional Medal of Honor. That supersedes anything I've done to date, I'd say."

"What do you mean?"

"Just what I said. Matthew Campbell will decorate you with the Medal as soon as you've recovered. Thank you for your bravery. You richly deserve this honor." He looked down his nose at Jax. "I don't believe that you, on the other hand, deserve my daughter. But I'll respect her wishes."

The blackened window swished up.

"Well, I'll take that limited endorsement." Jax hooted a laugh. "Let me get you closer to the car so I don't have so far to carry you."

At the passenger side of the truck, she ringed her arms around his neck. Jax eased her out of the chair, lifted her through the open front door and smoothly sat her in the leather seat. Both of them breathed heavily when he sat behind the wheel.

"Phew," he said. "We're a pair."

She stroked her hand over the dashboard. "Wow, Jax. I love this car. Thank you."

"You're welcome." He beamed at her, switched on the engine and put the car in reverse.

Back up beeps sounded as if alarm bells had triggered her brain to think things through. "Where are we going? To Grace's residence?"

"No. To your home. I packed my things at the Vice President's house this morning."

"Pretty cocky to assume I'd say yes," she teased.

"I had a plan B. Grace lined up a plane to take me back to Chicago just in case."

"Chicago… right. How will this work, Jax, with you there and me here? It may take me some time, but I'm returning to Grace's detail as soon as I'm fit. My base is here."

"Dryden has agreed to any arrangement that works for us. I can work remotely as much as I want. Maybe visit Chicago for meetings…or pleasure if you have time off. I'll keep my condo there."

"And move in with me?"

"If that's what you want. If not, I'll buy a place close by your home."

"First of all—I'm willing. Second of all, do you know how high real estate values have risen around here?"

He chuckled. "Well, that's not actually a problem. Seems I'm a multi-millionaire these days."

"Holy moly. How? Did you win the lottery or something?"

"Baxter deeded the mansion to my mother. Probably to hide assets, not out of any concern for his wife's well-being," he spat out. "Mom's lawyer sold the place for twenty mil and I'm her sole heir. So…"

"Well now I'm *really* glad that I said yes."

She switched on the radio to a country music station and hooted in delight when Josh Turner's voice filled the cabin. "Our song…"

Brooke leaned back in the comfortable seat, her heart winging. She replayed the dream that wasn't a dream in her mind. "You obviously heard me tell you I wanted a red Silverado instead of puppies or a pub."

"Yep. I did."

"Did you hear the part about how I wanted a ring, too?"

"Yep. Loud and clear."

"Well?"

"Check your glove compartment."

A word about the author…

K.M. Daughters is the pen name for team writers and sisters, Pat Casiello and Kathie Clare. The penname is dedicated to the memory of their parents, "K"ay and "M"ickey Lynch. K.M. Daughters is the author of 20 award winning romance genre novels. The "Daughters" are wives, mothers and grandmothers residing in the Chicago suburbs and on the Outer Banks, North Carolina. Visitors are most welcome at http://www.kmdaughters.com

Thank you for purchasing
this publication of The Wild Rose Press, Inc.

For questions or more information
contact us at
info@thewildrosepress.com.

The Wild Rose Press, Inc.
www.thewildrosepress.com

www.ingramcontent.com/pod-product-compliance
Lightning Source LLC
Chambersburg PA
CBHW070115260626
47160CB00004B/1477